"It isn't the tea that's raising my temperature,"

he told her. "From the very first time I saw you, I've wanted to do this."

"To do what?"

"To kiss you. To taste your mouth, to hold you and feel the strength under all that fragile softness."

He was coming closer. Breathlessly, she protested, "But that's crazy. It was only yesterday."

She waited, hardly able to support her own weight as a sweet weakness invaded her lower limbs.

Cyrus sighed. "Yesterday, huh? Funny, I thought it had been longer than that. We'd better wait until tomorrow, at least."

Dear Reader,

Welcome to Silhouette! Our goal is to give you hours of unbeatable reading pleasure, and we hope you'll enjoy each month's six new Silhouette Desires. These sensual, provocative love stories are both believable and compelling—sometimes they're poignant, sometimes humorous, but always enjoyable.

Indulge yourself. Experience all the passion and excitement of falling in love along with our heroine as she meets the irresistible man of her dreams and together they overcome all obstacles in the path to a happy ending.

If this is your first Desire, I hope it'll be the first of many. If you're already a Silhouette Desire reader, thanks for your support! Look for some of your favorite authors in the coming months: Stephanie James, Diana Palmer, Dixie Browning, Ann Major and Doreen Owens Malek, to name just a few.

Happy reading!

Isabel Swift
Senior Editor

DIXIE BROWNING
A Winter Woman

Silhouette Desire

Published by Silhouette Books New York

America's Publisher of Contemporary Romance

SILHOUETTE BOOKS
300 East 42nd St., New York, N.Y. 10017

Copyright © 1986 by Dixie Browning

ISBN: 0-373-05324-X

First Silhouette Books printing December 1986

America's Publisher of Contemporary Romance

Printed in the U.S.A.

Books by Dixie Browning

Silhouette Romance

Unreasonable Summer #12
Tumbled Wall #38
Chance Tomorrow #53
Wren of Paradise #73
East of Today #93
Winter Blossom #113
Renegade Player #142
Island on the Hill #164
Logic of the Heart #172
Loving Rescue #191
A Secret Valentine #203
Practical Dreamer #221
Visible Heart #275
Journey to Quiet Waters #292
The Love Thing #305
First Things Last #323
Something for Herself #381
Reluctant Dreamer #460

Silhouette Special Editon

Finders Keepers #50
Reach Out to Cherish #110
Just Deserts #181
Time and Tide #205
By Any Other Name #228
The Security Man #314

Silhouette Desire

Shadow of Yesterday #68
Image of Love #91
The Hawk and the Honey #111
Late Rising Moon #121
Stormwatch #169
The Tender Barbarian #188
Matchmaker's Moon #212
A Bird in Hand #234
In the Palm of Her Hand #264
A Winter Woman #324

DIXIE BROWNING,

one of Silhouette's most prolific and popular authors, has written over thirty books since *Unreasonable Summer*, a Silhouette Romance, came out in 1980. She has also published books for the Desire and Special Edition lines. She is a charter member of the Romance Writers of America, and her Romance *Renegade Player* won the Golden Medallion in 1983. A charismatic lecturer, Dixie has toured extensively for Silhouette Books, participating in "How To Write A Romance" workshops all over the country.

Dixie's family has made its home along the North Carolina coast for many generations, and it is there that she finds a great deal of inspiration. Along with her writing awards, Dixie has been acclaimed as a watercolor painter, and was the first president of the Watercolor Society of North Carolina. She is also currently president of Browning Artworks, Ltd., a gallery featuring fine regional crafts on Hatteras Island. Although Dixie enjoys her traveling, she is always happy to return to North Carolina, where she and her husband make their home.

Prologue

The first strains of the wedding march reached the back of the sanctuary, and Delle Richardson swayed. She clutched at her father's arm to brace herself.

"Steady, girl," C. R. said gruffly. "Your mother was just about as bad on our wedding day. It'll pass."

The altar looked a thousand miles away, as if seen through the wrong end of a telescope. Against banks of glossy dark greenery and pale blossoms, an array of figures stood stiffly. Waiting.

They neared the halfway point, and Delle's eyes leaped ahead, frantically searching out the pink-clad figure of her matron of honor as if she were a lifeline. *Hetty? Don't just stand there, do something!*

Jeanette, Delle's stepmother, had insisted she have eight attendants. Delle had wanted only her three best friends. They'd compromised on six, including Peter's three sisters.

Delle's gaze darted to the two tall figures on the right. Peter and her eldest brother, Oren. She closed her eyes, stumbled and felt her father's arm clamp her fingertips tightly against his side. "Watch it," he whispered without moving his lips.

Oh, God, she thought, she couldn't go through with this. She just couldn't do it! She was going to be sick to her stomach before she ever got as far as the altar.

Why had she let it get this far? Why hadn't she simply stood up to them last night?

The final deep notes of the organ rumbled into silence right on cue. Her father stepped away, and Peter took his place at her side. Delle clamped her elbows tightly against her body, trying not to breathe the sickening smell of roses and lilies. Under the cover of ivory silk and antique guipure lace, a bead of perspiration formed and began to trickle down her spine.

Hetty, get me out of here! she pleaded silently as she met the puzzled brown eyes of her dearest friend. Dr. Portman cleared his throat and stepped forward, smiling benignly down on the assembled wedding party. The church was filled to capacity with guests who had come to witness the marriage of Cordelia Reynolds Richardson to Peter Abbott Remington-Dunn. *Hurry, hurry, before it's too late!*

The musky scent of Peter's cologne reached Delle's nostrils, mingling uncomfortably with the scent of the flowers. Her stomach churned, and she crushed the bouquet of white orchids and stephanotis in damp, lace-mitted fingers and lifted her chin. It was now or never.

"Peter," Delle said in a trembling, but quite audible whisper to the man at her side, "You and Oren had better leave—use the choir door, it's closer. I'm not going to marry you, you know."

Then, twin patches of color in an otherwise colorless face, she turned to face the assembly.

One

____

The bumper-to-bumper traffic moved forward tentatively another few feet and stopped again. Delle's fingers tapped the steering wheel. Her cheeks felt cold, a sure sign that her eyes had been leaking again. They did that with alarming frequency these days—with no notice, and for no apparent reason. She gunned the engine impatiently, feeling the familiar burning sensation in the pit of her stomach. One of these days she was going to get herself a helicopter and be done with it. It would take two or three minutes at most from her office in the bank building to her new waterfront condo.

During the next ten minutes she crept forward another two blocks. What was the point of having 250 horses under the hood when a goat cart could get her home as quickly?

An hour later Delle checked the medicine cabinet, swore and then dug in her purse for the roll of antacid tablets she'd sent out for that morning. She consumed the last one, crumpled the foil and threw it at an alabaster wastepaper basket. She missed.

For a long moment she simply stared at the scrap of trash on her white carpet. Her eyes blurred, her nose began to sting, she swore again. It had been another one of those days when nothing had gone right. Why should things change now?

She fixed herself a drink, set it on the credenza and reached for the mail. The square taupe envelope on the top turned out to be only a handwritten note from her favorite dress shop telling her about a collection put together with her tastes in mind. "With my salary in mind, more likely," Delle grumbled.

There were several solicitations, two of which she put aside for later consideration, a bill from a restaurant where she regularly entertained clients and a pale gray envelope with a North Carolina postmark that was addressed in Hetty Sprague's distinctive scrawl. Delle groaned. Had another year gone by already? Surely the last reunion had been only a few weeks ago.

"You're not getting out of our annual Gulls' T-Potty this time," Hetty had written. "It's June's turn to pick a place, and she says think beach. I'll call as soon as we know for sure. Before you start making excuses, just remember that attending members get to talk about anyone who isn't there, so if you back out, you'd better have asbestos ears."

Delle unfastened the waistband of her skirt, slipped off her gray lizard pumps and collapsed onto the down-filled cushions of her new white tweed sofa. If gossip could burn, her ashes would have long since blown away. A covey of saints would have had a field day with what happened six years ago. Hetty, June and Paula were wonderful women and she loved them dearly, but they were no saints. All through boarding school and college the four of them had been together, and they had vowed after graduation to meet once a year, come feast or famine, husbands or children. They'd called the annual reunions after one of the less popular social customs of their dormitory, the mandatory weekly tea parties presided over by a housemother who referred to her young female charges as her "gulls."

This would be the seventh reunion since the year they graduated, the sixth since Delle's wedding—the wedding that hadn't quite taken place. The events of that day had never been mentioned, at least not in Delle's hearing, but she knew that despite her success, her friends were still convinced she was miserably unhappy.

Unhappy? That was a laugh. While the three of them were changing diapers, swabbing Pablum off the kitchen floor and car-pooling to play school and kindergarten, she'd been climbing to the top of her chosen field, dining out with heads of corporations, playing golf or cruising Norfolk's spectacular waterfront with a different client each weekend.

And *they* felt sorry for *her*?

The grandfather clock in Hetty Sprague's hall bonged four times. "The gulls' planning board had better come up with something before my rib roast has to go in the oven," Paula warned. She lived three blocks away from Hetty, in the same affluent neighborhood.

"I'm still waiting to hear if we can get that place at North Myrtle Beach," June reminded her. "Hetty, what did Howard say about the new broker in his firm? Do you think he'd be interested? How long has he been divorced? If we could invite the men down for a golfing weekend and include him, and sort of forget to tell Delle . . ."

"She'd walk out. Don't forget what she did the time we tried to fix her up with that dental surgeon."

"And the one before that," Paula added. "Lawsy, I thought I'd die when she told him point-blank that if he didn't keep his hands where they belonged, he'd be playing Beethoven with his elbows."

"Remember how sweet and shy she used to be?"

"Until that creep..."

"Yeah."

After several moments of silence, Paula sighed. "She can't be happy. All that golf... She's the only girl I know who flunked phys ed, and as for all that entertaining she claims she does, well I wonder."

"Nobody changes that much. Delle's idea of heaven used to be a midnight horror movie, a gallon of popcorn and no classes until noon the next day."

"Now it's expense account dinners and three martini luncheons."

"Delle hates martinis," Paula put in, a stickler for accuracy.

"Figure of speech." June said, dismissing the correction. "Look, I know we promised faithfully, no more men, but—"

"*You* promised," Hetty corrected. "Paula and I didn't say a word. Besides, it's for her own good," she added self-righteously. "This fellow in Howard's office I told you about last week, he's only been divorced a couple of months. What do you think? Too soon?"

"I don't know. He doesn't sound like her type."

Hetty shrugged. "He's male."

"He's dull."

"He's loaded."

"So's she."

Hetty sank back into her chair. "Yeah. Well. Back to the drawing board, ladies. But frankly, good men are getting to be scarce as hens' teeth. If they're worth having, they're already had. So to speak."

June leaned forward, her eyes narrowing on a new idea. "Wa-a-ait a minute, do you all remember that big art vandalism case a few years back? You know, this guy came home one night and caught these punks trashing his art collection?''

Two faces turned toward her, one dark and clever, the other round and freckled. Hetty spoke first. "Don't tell me, let me guess. They went to prison, one of them wrote a book that made him rich and famous, and now he's out on parole and hungry for love, right?''

Paula leaned back and crossed her plump arms behind her head. "Come to think of it, I've got a cousin somewhere around Myrtle Beach. Female, and I haven't seen her in years, but she might know an eligible man or two. Worth a try.''

"Forget Myrtle Beach," June said decisively. "Hetty, can I run up your phone bill?''

The third time Delle yelled at her secretary on Monday, Daniel yelled back. "Look, I don't know what's bugging you, but stop taking it out on me, will you? I do have feelings, you know.''

Delle turned to stare blindly out the window until she regained control of herself. Tears again, the same stupid tears that had plagued her so often these past few months. When she had herself under control once more, she turned to face the tall, dark-haired young man who stood stiffly beside her desk.

"Daniel, I'm sorry. I don't know why I yelled at you. I don't usually lose my temper.''

"It's not your temper, Ms. Richardson, that's a symptom, not the cause. Speaking of symptoms, you might read the fine print on those tablets you keep devouring. You're way over the maximum dosage.''

"Oh, for goodness sake, they're just antacids.''

"Why don't I make you an appointment for a physical?''

"Why don't you mind your own business? Am I seeing Beeker this afternoon or not? And see if you can get reservations at that place he likes for dinner, just in case there's something to celebrate."

Delle managed to get through the afternoon with no further lapses, but on his way out, Daniel reminded her that a physical might be in order.

"There's nothing wrong with my health, Daniel. I had a checkup seven months ago."

"Then take a vacation. One of us is going to have to, and I've already had my allotted two weeks."

Delle stayed at her desk long after everyone else in the building had left that evening. There had been nothing to celebrate. Beeker had obtained his five-million-dollar loan from two other banks, in spite of all the work she'd put in on the initial presentation and the follow-up.

Where had she gone wrong? Had she pushed too hard? Not hard enough?

Delle found it impossible to concentrate. In fact, she found herself dangerously close to not giving a damn, and that was scary.

At least traffic had thinned by the time she headed home. Her head was throbbing, but with her stomach on its usual late-afternoon rampage, she hesitated to take anything for her head. She'd always been prone to stomach trouble—well, not always, but for all her adult life. For the past several years, anyway.

Delle had bought the Marina Plaza condo because it was closer to the financial district than her old apartment had been, but after three months, it still looked like a decorator's showroom and smelled of paint and plaster. She was both frustrated and disappointed. She'd thought that some of the restlessness she'd been feeling lately might go away if she had a home of her own, a place where she could relax on the rare weekends when she wasn't entertaining.

It had crossed her mind that she might even get back into the nature photography she'd once enjoyed so much. A few sepia enlargements, something stark, yet soft, might look nice on all these bare walls.

Unfortunately, hobbies took time and energy, and she had neither. She either brought her work home or stayed late at the office on the few nights when she wasn't wining and dining a prospective client. Weekends were no better. Waterfront cruises, sight-seeing tours and golf. Delle *hated* golf, but it was more or less mandatory in her position. One of these days, she kept promising herself, she was going to gather enough courage to buck the tide and do business in her office instead of on a golf course.

Meanwhile, she was paying a fortune for a superb view that she seldom had time to enjoy, and a marvelous kitchen that she had no time even to explore, much less to use. Which might be a blessing in disguise, considering the fact that she'd never learned to cook.

Prominent woman banker poisons self with first home-cooked meal—she could see the headlines now.

One of these days she'd sign up for a course in French cookery, and one in photography where she'd have access to a darkroom. One day when she wasn't so tired. Currently she was either sleeping like the dead for ten hours straight, or lying awake reconsidering every decision she'd made throughout the business day.

Neither way brought much relief from the physical weariness that seemed to accumulate with each passing year. It really didn't add up. Oh, sure, she was overworked, but who wasn't? Her plan was going like clockwork, and that was the important thing. There wasn't a reason in the world why she shouldn't make senior vice president before she was thirty-five. She'd already talked to several headhunters from New York banks, and if she made the right moves at the right time, there was no reason why she couldn't make president by the time she was forty-five.

It would be worth it, if only to see the expression on her father's and Oren's faces. The thought was almost subliminal, so much a part of her nature had it become.

Eventually she found the energy to get undressed. She hung up her suit, dropped her silk blouse on a chair to go to the cleaners and, standing before the large mirror over her dresser, ruffled her thick, collar-length hair. Twenty-eight and not a single gray strand. Her hair was the same chestnut brown it had always been, just as thick, just as glossy. Funny how surface appearances could lie. Inside she felt withered and gray, but the reflection that stared back at her stood tall and straight, the skin that stretched over her firm jawline and rounded forehead, pale olive and unlined.

Acting on impulse, she suddenly crossed to the phone and punched a button on her automatic dialer. If she waited to think about it, she'd find a dozen good reasons to back out. Daniel was right, she did need a vacation.

"Hetty? Delle. Look, I got your note. Has June picked out a place yet?"

Five minutes later she hung up and fell back across the bed. She'd committed herself. Not for the whole week, but at least for a part of it.

Coranoke. Now all she had to do was find out how to get there.

She punched the fourth number down, the first three being emergency numbers. "Daniel? I'm taking off the second week in November."

"You're kidding! Remember that fellow from Edgemont's corporate trust group you've been trying for weeks to pin down? I've got a meeting set for November eighth."

"All right, after that, then."

"Look, why not take off the following week? Things will be all torn up around here while they install the new computers. I've kept the calendar clear for the whole week, because it's bound to be ghastly with all that noise and dust.''

"I've already made plans for the second week, but..." Delle closed her eyes for a moment, and then took the plunge. "Yes, I'll do it."

"I'll arrange it. Third week in—"

"No, the second *and* the third."

"Both of them? You must be planning something marvelous. Sure you don't need a male companion for protection?"

It wouldn't be the first time Daniel had served as her escort. He was charming and older women took to him, which left Delle free to discuss business with their husbands. He was an excellent secretary and a good friend, but that was all he was...or wanted to be.

"It's an island called Coranoke," she told him. "A few cottages, a few fishing boats, and that's about all, according to Hetty."

"Sounds utterly depressing. You'll be bored stiff inside twenty-four hours."

"So I'll drive back to Norfolk and fly up to New York for a few days. See what you can line up for me there, and I'll check with you later about reservations."

"Ready to make your big move?"

"Daniel," she said reproachfully. "You know I always take busman's holidays."

"Of course you do, but in case you're interested, I adore New York. Tell them you come fully equipped with your own staff. I think we can trade me up to a better title, don't you?"

As it turned out, it was Wednesday before Delle could get away from work. Daniel had postponed as many of her appointments as he could, but there were some that couldn't wait. Those he'd moved up to the first two days of the week.

She called Hetty to let her know and was assured that it didn't matter.

"We'll only talk about you a *little* bit," her friend promised. "And only in the nicest possible way. Once you get to Hatteras, just follow the signs to the ferry landing. The last one leaves for Coranoke at five-thirty."

Delle had planned to catch an earlier ferry, but by the time she'd stopped in Nags Head to stop for beach clothes and visited a few interesting looking shops on Hatteras Island, she almost managed to miss the last one. Her sleek navy BMW was the only car crossing the inlet, and Delle leaned against the railing, watching one island disappear as another one took shape against the setting sun.

It occurred to her that she hadn't needed an antacid tablet since she'd left home that morning.

The instructions had been simple enough: follow the paved road until you come to a gray shingled cottage with red-and-white storm blinds and a palm tree out front.

A palm tree? In North Carolina? Hetty wasn't notably horticultural; she'd probably meant a *pine* tree.

It was nearly dark by the time Delle found the cottage. The shingles were silvery gray, the storm blinds red-and-white, and the peculiar looking growth in the front yard was definitely a palm. Stunted, battered, probably moribund, but definitely a palm of some sort. Even so, Delle wondered if she could have made a mistake. There was no sign of Hetty's car out front.

They'd gone out to eat, she decided after a glance at her watch. She hadn't passed a restaurant, but there had to be one somewhere. This was still a resort, even if it was pretty far off the beaten track.

Leaving her bags in the car, Delle climbed the five wooden steps, crossed the wide porch and knocked. "Hetty? June? Paula? Brew the tea, I'm here!"

It was several moments before she saw the glimmer of white sticking out from the screen door. She slipped out the scrap of paper and squinted vainly in the dim light, finally giving in and taking it back to the car. Under the yellow glow of the courtesy light, she scanned the short note.

"I don't believe this," she wailed. An impacted wisdom tooth? Poor June!

"Settle in and enjoy," Hetty had written. "The green bedroom is yours, since you're the only nonsmoker and it's a single. Food in fridge, bar well-stocked, natives friendly. We may have to stay in Kitty Hawk overnight, but will call. Key inside screen door."

So much for the seventh annual Gulls' T-Potty, Delle mused as she transported one small suitcase and several shopping bags to the porch. A little guiltily, she acknowledged a faint sense of relief at having the cottage all to herself for a few hours. She needed the time to unwind and put herself into the proper frame of mind.

If things went as usual, they'd spend the first hour or so groaning about added pounds, graying hair and new wrinkles. They'd pull out snapshots for show-and-tell, and Delle would say the appropriate things about husbands' promotions and children's triumphs. It was fun, actually, once she got in the swing of it. The children were darlings and even the husbands were nice enough. Of course, Paula's husband had once made a pass at her, and June's Abner told off-color stories that weren't very funny. As for Hetty's Howard, he was dull as mud, but thoroughly decent. He adored Hetty, and that was what counted.

Family disposed of, they'd get on with the traditional gossipfest covering friends, former friends and classmates. Delle tossed her alumni letters into the wastebasket, but the others kept up with dozens of the women they'd gone to school with. All things considered, Delle decided, her three friends were much nicer than she was.

Except when it came time for, "Delle, when are you going to wise up and get out of the rat race?"

It never failed. No matter how much she protested—no matter how much they complained about being tied down and envying Delle her single life, every one of them was dedicated to finding her a husband.

"Oh, the devil with it." Retrieving the key, she unlocked the door and let herself inside, pausing to inhale the pleasant scent of wood paneling and furniture polish.

It didn't take long to see all there was to see. Delle unpacked the clothes she'd brought, and the new ones she'd bought along the way, and considered returning to the car for a bottle of wine. She decided it wasn't worth it. She could hardly hold her eyes open, as it was. One glass of wine and she'd be out like a light.

She truly wanted to stay awake in case there was a call, but after little more than an hour, she gave up. Something about the sound of surf washing against the shore made her eyelids incredibly heavy.

Her bedroom was simply furnished, the paneled walls painted the soft green of apple leaves, the wide pine floorboards graced with white crocheted rugs to match the white candlewick spread. There was a small pewter pitcher filled with colorful gaillardia blossoms on her dresser. June's touch. Knowing how she loved them, June always remembered Delle's birthdays with flowers.

She changed into her teddy, located a blanket, even though it wasn't really cold, and opened both windows to the soft, damp breeze. Her body seemed to melt and flow into the mattress, and lulled by the soothing sounds of the island, she was asleep within minutes.

At first she thought she was still dreaming. Plane after plane broke the sound barrier right over her head. Sonic booms, one after the other, rocked the house, bringing her bolt upright.

My God, what's happening? she thought with alarm. Clutching her pillow as protection, Delle slipped out of bed and made her way cautiously to the window, half afraid to open her eyes.

There was no drone of jet engines in the distance, no more sonic booms. No gunfire, no cannons. As far as she could see, the island wasn't being invaded. The wildflowers were still in their pitcher on the edge of the dresser, not flung across the floor. Which meant that it probably hadn't been an earthquake.

Could she have dreamed it? It wouldn't be the first time she'd suffered nightmares, but this one had seemed so real.

Delle crossed to the other window, where the view was essentially the same. The sky had a bleary look, as if the sun were still trying to make up its mind whether or not to get out of bed. Even in the dull light she could see that the cottage was nestled snugly in the center of a grove of live oaks, bays and pines.

Not a clue as to what could have roused her from such a sound sleep.

Yawning, she turned to climb back into bed, half convinced she'd had a particularly vivid dream, when the noise came again. *Boom, boom, boom!* Only this time it was sharper—more like *rap, rap, rap!*

Without a thought as to her skimpy attire, Delle charged out into the front yard, still clutching her pillow.

"All right, all right, that does it! What is going *on* around here?" she growled under her breath. Not until she neared the battered palm tree did she spot the ladder. It was centered between the two windows of her bedroom so that she couldn't possibly have seen it from either one.

A ladder?

Holding the pillow in front of her as if it were an armored shield, she scanned the length of the ladder until it
disappeared into the scraggly branches of a live oak tree that
brushed against the eaves.

The first thing that came into view was a foot. One well-
ventilated sneaker, topped by a portion of tanned ankle.
Even as she stared, the other foot descended into view,
bringing with it a length of muscular calf. Before she could
assimilate that much, one thigh, its contours softened by a
golden haze of body hair, and then a set of lean hips came
into view. Both sneakered feet paused on the rung for several moments, giving her time to consider the fact that
whoever belonged to the lower appendages didn't believe in
overdressing. If he was wearing anything at all under those
disgustingly brief torn-off jeans, it certainly wasn't visible
from where she stood.

Unconsciously, Delle moved closer to the base of the ladder, still gazing upward. The figure on the ladder shifted
suddenly, and something came sailing down from the roof,
striking the ground with a riflelike report. She yelped, and
the man on the ladder twisted around, peering through a
clump of glossy leaves.

"What the— Where the hell did you come from? Lady,
don't you know you can get hurt that way?"

"Do you have any idea what time it is? What if I'd had a
weak heart?" Shading her eyes against the hazy glare, Delle
tried to see past the bronze chest and shoulders. She couldn't
make out his features, but at least he was human. "I could
have been frightened into a heart attack!"

"If you'd been standing any closer, you could have been
driven six feet into the ground, too." The stack of shingles
he'd dropped had landed not far from where she stood.

Heaving a toolbox over the edge of the roof, he caught its
weight in one hand and proceeded to descend the ladder,
and Delle watched as if mesmerized. Judging from the way

eed anything. When no one had turned up by the middle
f the day, he had figured he could get those shingles re-
laced before the rains started. NOA weather radio was
alking about another low-pressure area forming off Hat-
ras, and those things had a tendency to hang around this
me of year.

The trouble was, the place had been booked solid since
pril. Like his other rental properties, it needed repairs that
d had to wait until the season ended. Still, at $750 a week,
wasn't complaining. One of the promises he'd made
mself when he started his venture was that it be self-
pporting. So far, he was right on target.

He lowered the ladder and left it alongside the house to
lect when he came back in the truck. Hefting the tool-
x, he set off through the woods at the back of the house,
lowing a barely discernible path.

Cyrus's house, the only one on the sound side, was simi-
to most of the dozen or so houses on the island. Made of
per shingles that had long since weathered to a pleasing
le of gray, it was simply constructed. It had been built
off the ground to avoid the tides that sometimes swept
the whole island, and it huddled in a grove of ancient
for protection against the fierce winds that battered the
during the winter months.

like the one he'd just left, his yard sported an assort-
of vehicles, small boats, drying nets and a stack of crab
hat needed repairs. Everything needed repairs. Thanks
proximity of the Gulf Stream, the weather was warm
nto the winter, but the mildness was deceptive. The
e was seldom as kind as it seemed.

ning the door of a rusty white pickup truck, he slid
olbox inside and jogged across the sandy yard to the
of his porch. There he shucked off his shoes, dumped
e sand and, leaving them neatly parked beside the
at, let himself inside.

his muscles flexed the box must weigh a ton. Good Lord,
what a body! Hadn't she seen him done in marble at the art
museum?

What was she thinking of? The man could have killed her,
and she was coolly evaluating his physique? "You could at
least have yelled 'timber.'"

"They're not wood, they're asphalt. What would you
have done if I'd yelled out, 'asphalt'?"

He came on down the ladder, and Delle's gaze strayed
from the hard calves that swelled as he centered a foot on
each rung in turn, to the neat buttocks that flexed with each
step and finally to a narrow waist that flared sharply to the
most beautiful back she'd ever seen on a man. Not gro-
tesquely muscular, but shapely and strong, and as smooth
as polished bronze.

Her bare toes curled into the sand, and she swallowed
hard. Not until he reached the ground and turned to confront her did she remember that she'd jumped out of bed
and dashed out without a thought to anything but getting
out from under before the sky fell.

"Hel-lo," the man drawled, surveying her with discon-
certing thoroughness. "Where did you come from, anyway?"

Covering the front of her brown satin teddy with the pillow, Delle adopted her frostiest corporate tone. "I came
from inside this house. Would you mind telling me what you
were doing hammering on the roof in the middle of the
night?" She was trying to make up her mind whether or not
the face went with the rest of the body. It certainly wasn't
the sort one would ever see on a Roman coin. As for the
marble at the museum, she couldn't even remember what its
face looked like. So much for culture.

"Cyrus Burrus." He extended a hand, and after a slight
hesitation, Delle cautiously entrusted him with hers. His
palm felt like leather.

"Cordelia Richardson. Is there some reason why you're here?"

"Is there some reason why *you're* here?" A series of small changes took place in his weathered face, and Delle watched in fascination. It was mostly the eyes, she decided—they were like multifaceted green gemstones. Not emeralds, but something more subtle. They fairly danced with light.

Her head snapped back. She was definitely losing her grip—actually standing here with an insolent, near-naked handyman, examining the quality of his smile! "I think if you go back and look at your work order you'll find that you've come to the wrong address," she said courteously. "This cottage is rented until the end of the week."

The green gemstone eyes—peridot, she decided—were hidden behind a sweep of thick, surprisingly dark lashes. "Ma'am, on Coranoke we don't have addresses. We have Up the Road, Down the Road, Out and Over."

"I beg your pardon?"

"There's only one paved road, the one that goes from the ferry landing to the dock. If you live near the ferry landing, you live Up the Road. If you live closer to the dock, you live—"

"Let me guess," she said dryly. "Down the Road."

"You're catching on. The sand road that runs past the store bisects the island about midway. There's only one house on the sound side. That's Over. There aren't any houses at all on the ocean side, but that's Out. It's no different from anywhere else. You could say let's go *up*town, or *down*town, or *over* to the parkway or *out* to the shopping center. We just don't happen to have those particular amenities."

"If Abbott and Costello had heard about this they'd have been famous," Delle said dryly. Her attention strayed to his hair, which was thick with a layered look—golden on top,

smoky brown beneath. She knew women who paid a tune for just that effect. His was probably natural.

"Look, all I'm saying is you must have the wrong she explained with rapidly eroding patience. "I kn fectly well that whoever rented this house to my wouldn't have arranged to have repairs done withou ing us. What if I'd had a weak heart? There's no telli might have happened, and it would all be your faul

"On the other hand, what if *I'd* had a weak he returned. "Can you imagine climbing down a thinking you're completely alone, and finding practically falling into the arms of a feather dance

"A feather—?"

"And here I thought they only went in for pi plumes and peacock fans," Cyrus said admirin subtle approach has a lot more class."

A strangled sound escaped Delle's throat as curled into the down pillow. Spinning around, to the door. She could feel his laughing eyes f every step of the way, but if she'd been offered board of Chase Manhattan, she wouldn't have step. Let him stare, dammit! What was that c a commoner being able to look at a king? It a to handymen and vice presidents.

With the eyes of a connoisseur, Cyrus watch round the corner. Impeccable lines. God, sh He didn't know what she was doing here, particularly care as long as she stayed. Let roof leak like a sieve, let the walls sprout bro every crack.

The other three had left yesterday...so toothache and a change of plans. The Spr said someone else would stay the rest of should stop by frequently to make sure

He'd take time for a cup of coffee, and then he might take the Blazer and run out to his favorite slough on the north beach to see if there was any action. Commercial fishing had been off lately, and he was getting fish hungry.

Cyrus poured himself a cup of the coffee he'd made earlier and took it into the living room. His furniture was mostly leather covered, easy to keep clean for someone who was usually either wet or sandy or both. There was a Navaho rug over the back of the couch, another one hanging on the paneled wall. The rest of the walls, those that weren't taken up with windows, were covered with bookshelves and paintings.

Cyrus appreciated beauty in all its forms. When he'd decided to simplify his life, he hadn't made the mistake of getting rid of all the things that brought him pleasure: his stereo equipment, a library of records and tapes, his art collection—or what was left of it. His bookshelves sagged under the weight of hundreds of volumes, from reference books to his favorite classics, to mass market-paperbacks. His home was always open to the boys. It was a calculated risk, one he felt he had to take.

"Cordelia Richardson," he murmured, closing his callused hands around a heavy mug. "Now where the devil did she drop from?"

A slow smile kindled in his eyes and spread to his lips. More to the point, how long was she going to be around? He'd postpone repairs indefinitely if he could talk her into hanging around for another few days.

The cottage had been reserved by Abner Gavins's wife. He'd known the Gavinses slightly when he'd lived in Charlotte, but he was pretty certain he'd never met Cordelia Richardson. He'd have remembered.

He'd done a lot of socializing back in those days, not all of it for business purposes. Thanks to his mother's family, he'd had all the advantages, belonged to all the right clubs, but it hadn't been enough. After awhile, it had begun to pall. The older he'd grown, the more he'd felt like a ship without a rudder, without ballast.

He'd found his bearings, all right, and he'd never once regretted changing the whole course of his life. But Coranoke was hardly paradise. One of the things he'd missed the most was the company of an attractive, intelligent woman.

A few of the bachelors in these parts had developed a practice he couldn't condone, even if he'd had the opportunity. In spring, just before the influx of tourists, they broke off with their women in order to be free for the summer crop of available talent. Then, as sure as the snowbirds headed south, they'd make it up with the local ladies to insure having a warm bed all winter.

Just because he'd given up his profession and his old way of life didn't mean he'd forsworn all the pleasures. Still, he hadn't reached the point of arranging his love life according to the season.

Two

The first full day of her vacation, and she was up at the crack of dawn. At this rate, she might as well not have bothered to come. Delle adjusted the shower until it ran several degrees colder than body temperature. She slipped off her teddy, her mind still on the exasperating events of the past few minutes. At least she hadn't had an audience. If any of her friends ever found out that she'd run screaming out the door like Henny Penny, wearing nothing but her pinfeathers, she'd never hear the last of it. It was bad enough that she'd made a fool of herself before a stranger.

But what a stranger! For the first time in her life, Delle could almost understand why a woman might enjoy watching a performance by a male exotic dancer. Even in the state she'd been in, she'd hardly been able to take her eyes off the man who'd climbed down from the roof. As an art, descending a ladder didn't require a whole lot of talent, and there'd been nothing even faintly exotic about the scrap of faded denim he'd been wearing, but that hadn't seemed to matter.

All things considered, Delle mused, hers was a surprising reaction for a woman who spent most of her waking hours in the company of some of the most successful men in business. Whether facing her across a boardroom table, enjoying a dinner at one of the best restaurants in town or showing off their prowess on the links, they left her stone cold. Every one of them. Even the eligible ones.

Then along came a half-naked laborer with holes in his sneakers, calluses on his palms and a face that might have been put together from spare parts, and she was practically drooling.

What did that make her? Depraved?

"Deprived is more like it," Delle muttered as she took a deep breath and darted under the shock of cool water. Her body swiftly compensated with a rush of heat. Once her brain started functioning again, it occurred to her to wonder why she was torturing herself awake this way. After all, she was on vacation. If she was smart, she'd go back to bed until the others arrived. They'd be up talking half the night tonight.

After getting dressed, she wandered restlessly about the cottage. It was certainly nothing fancy, but all in all, she much preferred it to the time-share condo in the mountains where they'd gone the year before last. The communal courts, links, and pools had been too much like work for Delle's taste. She'd grown up a member of a country club where it was a point of honor to claim business as an excuse for belonging. Now she herself was a member of another such club, purely for business reasons.

Aside from the three bedrooms and two baths, the cottage had a large open area that combined kitchen, dining and living space. The walls were paneled in what looked and smelled like cedar, and the unpretentious furnishings were brightened by the addition of a few decoys, a model sail-boat and a shelf full of well-worn paperbacks. The screened porch that opened off the back obviously served as additional living quarters, weather permitting. Delle could have spent the entire week in the hammock that was strung across one corner.

By midmorning there was still no word, and she began to fidget. An impacted wisdom tooth was no picnic, and evidently it had started giving trouble shortly after they had arrived. They hadn't even had time to leave their mark on the cottage yet. All the other bedrooms were pristine. Hetty usually left a trail of dirty ashtrays, and Paula left magazines open to half-read articles in every room, warning everyone not to lose her place. With June, it was candy wrappers. The year before last she'd been hooked on fireballs, last year it had been M & Ms. This thing with the dentist might put an end to that.

Delle stared at the phone and willed it to ring. She hated being pinned down, waiting for a call with no idea when, or even *if*, it would come. Where was Daniel when she needed him? Her secretary would have told her to get out of the office for a breather and let him handle her calls. He looked after her like a mother hen in spite of the fact that he was two years younger, ordering lunch for her if she didn't have a luncheon appointment and then seeing that she ate it.

He scolded her for taking too many antacid tablets, but he was the first to sympathize when she ran head-on into a stone wall—including the stone wall of prejudice against women in her position. There were still a few unenlightened corporate financial officers who refused to deal with a woman.

She'd have to remember to tell Daniel that she'd gone two whole days without one of her tablets. In her rare self-pitying moods, she sometimes told herself that her secre-

tary was the only person in the whole world who really cared
about her.

Of course, Hetty, June and Paula *cared*, but that was
different. They had their own families, their own lives. The
three of them had always lived within a few miles of one
another in Charlotte, while Delle lived hundreds of miles
away, first in Richmond, then in Norfolk. Their lives since
graduation had taken wildly different directions, but the
bond between them had endured.

Not one of them had ever made a play for one of Delle's
brothers. That alone was enough to set them apart. Once it
had been discovered that she had three tall, dark and hand-
some older brothers, Delle had achieved instant popularity
with the girls at school.

Even then she'd been merely a means to an end.

Wandering to the front door, Delle peered out, hoping for
a glimpse of Hetty's car. She felt so restless, waiting for
them to come back so that her vacation could begin, waiting for them to call.... Waiting, waiting, waiting.

She *hated* waiting. It made her nervous. Her entire life
had been structured, from the time when she'd juggled
piano lessons, dancing lessons and kindergarten to the time
when she'd juggled night classes and her first responsible
position. Without a tight schedule, she tended to fall apart.

She had to get out of there. A watched phone never rang.
Impulsively, she tore off a scrap of notepaper and scribbled
a few lines.

Dear Gulls,
I've gone exploring. Unless I fall off the edge of the
world, I'll be back when I get hungry. There's an exotic strain of golden-crested *handimanus hunkus*
around these parts that Miss Binford never told us
about. Not sure about mating habits, but roosts on
rooftops. Keep your field guides and binoculars handy.
                                                    Love, Delle

P.S. If you'd sent me something like that instead of all those dull business types, I'd probably still be a teller in a branch office in outer Poquoson.

She left the note in a conspicuous place, stuffed a dollar in her pocket and then hid her purse in a battered double boiler in a kitchen cabinet. Evidently, things were pretty relaxed around here, but there was no point in making it too easy.

The minute she stepped outside, Delle could hear the ocean. It sounded as if the pines were sighing in rhythm with the beat of the surf. The air felt damp, but it was a nice dampness, almost balmy.

What was it Cyrus Burrus had said? Up, Down, Out and Over. By remembering which way she'd come from the night before, she quickly sorted Up from Down, but she hadn't the foggiest notion where Out and Over were.

Not that it really mattered. She was surrounded by water. If she followed the narrow strip of blacktop until she came to a crossroad and turned off in either direction, she was bound to come to... something. Besides, if she knew exactly where she was going, she wouldn't be exploring, and she needed the challenge.

In white rayon slacks, a cocoa-and-white V-necked polo, with a cocoa flax overshirt, she was drenched with perspiration before she ever reached the crossroad. She was also being eaten alive by mosquitoes, and her new white sandals were slowly amputating the little toes of both feet. To top it off, she was beginning to wonder if the natives were friendly.

The few houses she passed were uniformly compact, all huddled among the trees as if for protection against the wind, and all built high off the ground. She would have liked to think it was to catch any stray breeze in the summertime, but she suspected there was another reason. A few of the yards sported gleaming white dories. Nets were strung like enormous cobwebs between trees that, as often as not, had been neatly whitewashed halfway up the trunk.

Here and there a dour fisherman looked up from his net-mending to watch her stride past. She offered each one a friendly smile. Her greetings were gravely returned. "How do," unaccompanied by a smile, seemed the universal response. They watched her out of sight, and as a pale and watery sun surrendered to the thickening clouds, Delle's determined cheerfulness began to falter.

She reached the crossroad, a sandy rutted affair marked by a small one-room store literally covered with rusted metal signs. On the opposite corner was a weathered church pew, its carved surface silent evidence of generations of whittling observers.

She could picture them there, watching everyone who came and went at the little store, nodding and mumbling their gruff how-dos. What *was* it with these people? Was Cyrus just like the rest of them, glum, suspicious and close-mouthed? He certainly hadn't struck her that way, but then, perhaps if she'd paraded down Coranoke's main street in her brown satin teddy, those fishermen might have looked a little more lively, too.

The store was evidently a last outpost, and Delle decided that if she was going in search of the ocean, she'd better have something to drink first. She never bothered with breakfast, and this morning she hadn't even made coffee Lately the first few cups had tended to disagree with her Climbing the steps, she visualized herself in pith helmet and backpack, with canteens and compasses flapping about her hips.

"Morning."

The voluntary greeting took her by surprise. She gazed around at walls lined with shelves of canned goods that looked as if they might have been there since the Hoover administration. The floors were a dull shade of nothing, a cast-iron stove claimed pride of place in the center of the room, and behind the darkly varnished counter stood the female counterpart of all the stoic net-menders Delle had passed this morning.

"Good morning," she replied. "Do you have any cold drinks?"

The woman nodded to a rusted drink box in a corner, and Delle lifted the lid and made her selection.

"Skeeters bad," the woman ventured.

Skeeters? Mosquitoes, Delle translated, and yes, they were dreadful. "Are they always this bad?" she asked.

"Wind's been blowin' 'em off'n the mainland. Be better directly."

"By then they'll have picked my bones clean."

"I got some spray."

"I'll take it. Oh, I forgot. All I have with me is a dollar."

"Goin' far?" The woman's expression had not varied as far as Delle could see, except for her eyes. They were a lovely shade of blue-gray, and just as in Cyrus's case, they seemed to shimmer with a warm light that brought to mind the sound of laughter.

"I was trying to find the ocean. I got in after dark last night, and I'm still a little mixed up about my directions."

"Driving or walking?"

"Walking."

"I'd better spray you down then. They'll eat you alive till you get out o' the woods, but once you hit the beach, you'll be all right." She took an aerosol can from beneath the counter and led the way to a spot near the screened door. "Wind shifted in the night. Means more rain, but I reckon the good Lord knows what he's doin'. Leastways He waited till Cyrus got my gutters mended."

Delle covered her nose and eyes and allowed herself to be sprayed with a strong-smelling repellent. It would probably melt her new outfit before she got home, but better that than collect any more of the itchy lumps that were beginning to pop out on every exposed part of her body.

"How much do I owe you?" she gasped when she could breathe again. She paid for the drink, but the woman would take nothing for the spray.

"Free sample. If them bites gets to botherin' you, put a little bakin' soda in your bathwater."

Delle promised, but her mind was more on finding the ocean and then getting herself back to the cottage before the bottom fell out. After suffering this far, she was darned if she was going to give up now just because of threatened rain.

She went only a few steps before bending to remove her sandals. November was a little late in the year to be going barefoot, but cold toes were better than no toes at all. A few minutes ago, she'd actually been too warm, but the breeze seemed to have picked up slightly. She only hoped it would blow the mosquitos back where they came from.

Padding along the hard-packed sand, Delle finished her drink and looked for a place to stash the bottle until she came back. One bush seemed to stand out from the others, and so she left both bottle and sandals behind it. Not that she was particularly worried about anyone taking her sandals. So far, she seemed to be the only tourist on the island.

The thought brought surprisingly little comfort. Could it be that everyone else knew something she didn't?

Shortly after that, the road fanned out into myriad tracks across a barren stretch of sand. In the distance, a low line of dunes marked the nearness of the ocean, and Delle paused to catch her breath. Then, choosing a particular dune as a goal, she set off again. Some ten minutes later she trudged to the top and gazed down on the restless surf, feeling as triumphant as if she'd just discovered a new trade route to the Orient.

The sky was now leaden gray, the horizon lost in what she took to be fog. Close in, the sea was a paler shade of gray, laced with a fringe of white. By contrast, the sand looked quite pink, and Delle thought she'd never seen anything so lovely in her life. There was a subtlety about it that appealed to her enormously, and she was glad she was alone this first time. Hetty would have complained about the change in the weather, June would have wondered where all the people were, and Paula—Paula wouldn't have come along at all. She'd have been curled up back at the cottage with a stack of mysteries, a drink and a jar of salted nuts.

Delle breathed deeply of the pungent, iodine smell of seaweed. Lifting her arms over her head, she stretched, yawned unexpectedly and then flopped over from the waist, allowing her fingertips to trail in the sand. She felt marvelous! Mosquito bites, blistered toes and all, she couldn't remember the last time she'd felt so utterly relaxed.

As usual, Daniel was right. Things had been piling up all year, and she'd desperately needed to get away. Delle knew perfectly well she was courting an ulcer; unfortunately, it went with the territory. The pressure of constantly competing with loan officers from other banks was never-ending. Add to that the fact that, while some banks were highly supportive of women executives, hers was still largely a bastion of male supremacy, and the pressure compounded daily.

A woman invading a man's world had her work cut out for her under the best of circumstances, but even that hadn't been enough. Delle had a timetable. Six years ago she'd made her plans, setting certain goals and definite time limits. She prided herself that she was right on schedule.

It had taken Oren, her eldest brother, three and a half months longer than she to make vice president of his bank in Richmond. Both Wortham and Jonathan, her other two brothers, had gone directly into Richardson International, and as far as Delle was concerned, nepotism disqualified them altogether. Wortham was a wimp, and Jonathan's wonderful marriage had turned out to be not so wonderful, after all. Considering what the men in her family had tried to do to her, Delle couldn't find it in her heart to offer much sympathy.

By the time the rain started, she'd walked more than two miles along the shore. It began with a flurry of big drops that immediately turned into a hard, driving rain, pelting her skin and plastering her clothes to her body. She was quickly chilled to the bone. Splashing through the surf, which felt surprisingly warm, she jogged back the way she'd come, scanning the low woods for an opening.

Where *was* it? It was as if someone had smudged the horizon with a dirty thumb, erasing every detail.

Oh, great! She could see herself circling the island for days on end, looking for a way to get in to the center. Still, if she went far enough along the shore, she'd have to come to either the ferry landing or the dock. From there she could surely find her way back to the cottage. Probably.

Possibly, she amended, shivering in earnest now.

The vehicle almost ran her down before she saw it. Bristling with rods, it loomed up out of the rain and came to a halt a few feet away. Cyrus Burrus leaned out the open side and called to her, "Come on, hop in before you drown!"

Delle needed no urging. Running around to the passenger side of the rusted hulk on balloon tires, she grabbed the back of the seat, only to have it tip toward her. The darned thing wasn't even attached to the floor! Cyrus leaned across and held out his hand, and she took it and hauled herself inside. If it could be called inside. There was a roof of sorts but no doors, and the part that extended behind the front seat was more like an open back porch than anything else.

Still, it was better than nothing. "Thanks," she panted. "Lucky for me you happened along."

"Yeah." Cyrus downshifted and they lurched ahead, grinding through the sand, bouncing over ruts. Delle grabbed the plywood dashboard with both hands. She looked down and saw the ground passing under her feet, closed her eyes and took a tighter grip. The floor was a lacy network of rust. There were no seat belts, but then, what good was a seat belt when the whole seat was apt to fall through the floor at any moment?

"I left my shoes and a bottle beside the road." It was hard to speak when her teeth were clenched.

"Where?"

"Behind a bush."

Cyrus spared her a look that made her feel defensive when she had nothing whatsoever to feel defensive about. They'd come to the road again, and Delle peered at the wall of low shrubs that lined both sides of the sandy trail.

"I think it was...that one." She pointed slightly ahead of where they were, but by the time she'd finished speaking, they'd passed it and she knew it had been the wrong bush. "One sort of like it, with gray berries and sort of warm, olive-green leaves. Maybe that one." She pointed. "Or that one sticking up."

"Ms. Richardson, there are approximately 734 wax myrtle bushes lining the road between the beach and the crossroad. Suppose you tell me what's different about the one we're supposed to find?"

"Well, it has a pair of white sandals and an empty pop bottle behind it," she supplied meekly. Shoulders braced against the chills that were beginning to rack her body, she was growing more miserable by the moment. Being made to feel like a fool, especially twice in one morning, was not an experience she particularly enjoyed.

They picked up speed again, and Delle wrote off one pair of Italian sandals, purchased the day before expressly for this vacation. Add to that a slack suit that would probably never be the same, and she was already out a bundle. Great beginning. At least with a start like this, things couldn't get much worse.

"The cottage roof still leaks," Cyrus informed her as he pulled up behind her car.

"How do you know?"

"I checked it. Two places in the kitchen and another one in the back bedroom. I think it might be coming in around the flashing and running along the rafters. If it's gone as far as the outside wall, I'll have to take out some paneling to check for damp rot."

"But not this week. Surely a few more days can't matter."

Cyrus shrugged. He still wore the holey sneakers and the torn-off jeans, but he'd put on a faded navy sweatshirt. Wet, his hair looked almost as dark as hers. "Depends. The forecast calls for rain until the weekend. Personally, I think they're wrong, but in case they're right—"

"Terrific. Just what I need to make my beach vacation complete."

"If the insulation gets soaked, a lot of damage can be done in a week."

But Delle had forgotten all about the rain and any possible complications. She'd just remembered the note she'd left lying out where it wouldn't be missed. "Uh—you said you checked. Does that mean you actually went inside?"

"It's the only way I know of to tell if a roof leaks," Cyrus said mildly. "Why? You object to my letting myself in while you're not there?"

The rain drummed deafeningly on the top of the stripped Blazer. She couldn't very well ask him if he'd read her note. For all she knew, he might not even be able to read. There were a lot of functional illiterates around, and she hadn't seen any sign of a school on the island. At least this one had found his niche. He was gainfully employed, for which she gave him credit.

"Is it my imagination, or has it turned much colder?" she chattered with determined brightness.

"Wind shifted to the northeast early this morning. Temperature's dropping, but it won't get really cold."

"Yes, well, really cold is one thing when you're warm and dry, but I'm going to turn into an ice cube if I sit here another minute. Cyrus, thanks for the ride. I'm glad you happened along."

"Glad to oblige," he murmured, ducking his head in a polite nod.

It wasn't really laughter she saw in those green eyes of his, Delle decided. It was a trick of the light. Even if he'd read the note, he couldn't have understood it. The bird-watching bit referred to a camp counselor they'd once had who'd spent more time watching a certain male bird-watcher than she had the birds. The four girls had all known about it, and at thirteen, they'd thought it was a scream.

A hot bath, that was what she needed, Delle told herself as she slid down from the high seat to the ground. A deep, hot soak and a glass of sherry. After that, she'd wrap herself in the warmest clothes she could find and see if there was something canned in the kitchen she could open and heat. If not, she'd be reduced to cold sandwiches. Provided there was something to make them of.

An open fire would be nice, but she wasn't prepared to tackle the fireplace yet. At least the heating system was quick and efficient, she acknowledged a few minutes later. Peeling off layers of wet clothing, she hurried through to the bathroom, letting them lie where they fell. This was an emergency, and in cases of emergency, neatness didn't count. After adjusting the water, she flipped the lever to close the drain and went to see if there was any sherry. Hetty usually brought that and a liqueur, June brought all the mixers, Paula the hard stuff, and Delle supplied the table wine. It was still in the trunk of her car.

She sniffed the opened bottle, poured herself a generous glass and hurried back to the bathroom, now clouded with steam. Unfortunately, she'd forgotten to close the drain.

Or had she? Funny, she could have sworn she'd flipped that lever. She jiggled it, and nothing happened. She tried both positions, up and down, and neither worked. The chrome disk stayed right where it was, approximately an inch above the hole down which all her lovely hot water was disappearing.

Swearing, Delle shut off the water. She took a swallow of the sherry and sat down on the edge of the tub, only to yelp as her bare flesh touched the cold porcelain. Where were all the plumbers around here? Did everything on this blasted island leak?

Finally, she stuffed a washcloth into the hole as tightly as she could, turned on the water again and stepped in. It was better than nothing, she supposed, but she'd have to hurry before it leaked out. She'd counted on lying there sipping her sherry, drizzling more hot water in to keep the temperature up until she began to thaw out. The water wasn't leaking out as fast as she'd feared, but it wasn't very warm. Of course it took a lot of hot water to take the chill off these old-fashioned porcelain tubs. Either that or...

"Darn!" She twisted the valves shut. What was coming from the faucet was barely lukewarm. Evidently she'd used all the hot water. "Next time *I'm* picking the spot," she vowed. "A four-star hotel with room service and steam heat and a hot tub in every room!"

Twenty minutes later, Delle shook her head in disgust. "Capers, garlic, olive oil, ripe olives, anchovies, balsamic vinegar." She continued to name the contents of the pantry as her stomach growled in disappointment. Hetty loved doing exotic things with seafood. She'd brought along all the trappings, only where was the seafood? And where was the chef? There wasn't even any peanut butter!

Delle scratched a mosquito bite and wandered in to the living area to look through the phone book for the nearest restaurant. No breakfast, no lunch, and at this rate, no dinner, either. To make matters infinitely worse, she discovered a few moments later, all the restaurants seemed to be on Hatteras or Ocracoke. And the last ferry ran at five-thirty.

This was ridiculous. This was impossible! What had June been thinking about to book them into a place like this? It was hardly even civilized.

There were thirty-odd Burruses in the phone book, but only one Cyrus A. She dialed the number. He was probably out hammering on someone's roof. Or fishing. Or mending nets and grunting out unintelligible greetings to unfortunate tourists.

"Cyrus!" she blurted as soon as the connection was made. "Delle Richardson. Look, I hate to bother you, but you're the only one I know to ask. I must have an old phone book. I can't find a restaurant listing for Coranoke, and then I tried to look up the store, but I couldn't remember the name of it."

"It's just the store. The owner's name is Lavada Scarborough, but she doesn't have a phone, anyway."

"What about a restaurant?"

"Not on Coranoke, but if you want to run over to Hatteras, I can recommend a few."

"I don't. I'm too hungry to wait for a ferry now, and if I go for dinner, I'll have to spend the night. What sort of a system do you people have around here, anyway? It's totally inefficient."

"Oh, I don't know, I reckon that all depends on what your aims are. We seem to have accomplished ours."

"You're not helping, Cyrus!" The way her stomach was burning, she wouldn't be able to eat a bite, which only made things worse. How had she got herself in this fix? "I don't know why I ever agreed to come here in the first place. This so-called vacation has been awful from the word *go*."

"Sorry. If there's anything I can do, you have only to ask."

"Oh, forget it," she said morosely. "It's my fault, not yours." She hung up the phone and considered whether to get dressed and drive to the store for canned soup or to see what she could make with the contents of the refrigerator.

Returning to the refrigerator, Delle inventoried the contents and sighed in defeat. The freezer compartment revealed a two-pound package of ground round, frozen as solid as marble. The meat keeper boasted an evil-looking sausage coiled into striking position. It might or might not be ready-to-eat. Without knowing, she didn't care to experiment. Besides that, there was a bottle of tonic water, a big box of mushrooms that were already beginning to darken and three bunches of green onions.

She was still there when the back door opened to admit Cyrus and a large, brown paper bag. He was dripping wet and grinning apologetically as he glanced down at the clumps of wet sand he'd tracked in. "Thought it might slack off, but it's started in again."

Delle closed the refrigerator. "How did you get here? I didn't hear you drive up."

"Came through the back way. Can't do it in the summertime, ticks would be all over you, but this time of year I can outrun them."

"As I was saying, the charm of this place somehow escapes me. Ticks, mosquitoes, what other forms of livestock do you have that I ought to know about?"

Cyrus put the wet bag on the counter just before it disintegrated. From it he removed a jar of something silvery, half a loaf of rye bread and several mysterious foil-wrapped packets. "They caught a big gator over on Hatteras a few years back, but I wouldn't worry too much about those. They're rare in these parts. Outside of a few cottonmouths, some otters and muskrats, and a multitude of insects, Coranoke's wildlife is mostly the feathered variety. Long about the end of next month we'll be overrun with Audubon types doing the annual count. You a bird-watcher?"

Delle stole a wary glance at him. So he *had* read the note. And now he thought she was either a fool or a woman on the make, and he wasn't above taking advantage of it. Oh, terrific, that was just what she needed to make her stay complete!

"Like smoked mackerel? Lavada does these. We trade favors." He held up the jar, turning it so that the light reflected from the neatly arranged filets. "This is my last jar. I wouldn't share it with just anyone."

"You certainly don't have to share it with me. I wasn't hinting, Cyrus."

"Of course you weren't, but I was about to make myself some lunch when you called. Least I can do to make up for our lack of amenities," he offered generously.

There was simply no way she could refuse without seeming ungracious, and regardless of her other shortcomings, Delle's manners had always been impeccable.

Three

————

Polishing off the remnants of her lunch half an hour later, Delle stared thoughtfully at the man seated across the table. "You stack a mean sandwich, Cyrus. I'm impressed."

"Is that good or bad?"

"It's good. In fact, it was great. It reminds me of bagel and lox minus the bagel, without the lox, but with a few scrumptious extras."

The angular planes of his face shifted into a modest smile. "Purely a matter of survival."

Delle doubted it. Survival was a can opener and a microwave. Survival was the chicken nuggets and potato salad she could pick up on the way home from work on the rare nights when she didn't dine out. The composition of delicately smoked fillets, thinly sliced red onions, tiny tender spinach leaves and rye bread, all drizzled with herbed butter and dusted with freshly ground pepper, had been put together with a sure and discriminating touch.

On the other hand, perhaps she was giving him too much credit. Fish and onions on rye was hardly an unusual combination for an itinerant handyman who lived alone on an island where fish were plentiful.

Did he live alone? What had made her jump to that conclusion? Delle toyed with several versions of the same question and decided on the direct approach. "Are you married, Cyrus?"

He shook his head. "No. Are you?"

She shook her head quickly. In her capacity as a loan officer, Delle was accustomed to asking questions, not to answering them. At least not questions of a personal nature. When any of the men she dealt with showed signs of wanting to broaden their relationship—and it happened now and then—she had a courteous put-down that left them slightly stunned, but still in a negotiating frame of mind. It was a delicate act, and now and then it backfired on her, but for the most part, it was effective enough.

"I was only trying to make polite conversation," she said, and then cringed. Dear Lord, she hadn't actually said that, had she? And she prided herself on her tactfulness?

"Don't feel obligated to make conversation with me, Delle. I'm used to being alone. I can go whole days without saying a word."

Was he trying to tell her that he could do without her company? Or that he was lonely? If a man with Cyrus's looks was lonely, Delle realized, it was probably a matter of choice. She knew women in Norfolk who'd give a small fortune to be in her shoes right now.

"What else do you do besides mend roofs and gutters?" Delle closed her eyes. She was doing it again! Patronizing, condescending— Perhaps foot in mouth disease was endemic on the island.

If Cyrus took offense, he hid it well. Reaching across to her plate, he picked up a sliver of raw spinach that had fallen from her sandwich and nibbled on it with strong, white teeth. "I dabble in plumbing, simple carpentry, fish a few nets, run a few crab pots. In the summertime, I do some...uh, baby-sitting."

Baby-sitting? "Sort of a jack-of-all-trades, then," Delle said weakly.

He shrugged, drawing her eyes to his well-developed shoulders. "Call it self-reliance. Used to be a way of life down here a few generations back. Still is for some of us. Fishing, hunting, growing a few collards, maybe a bed of oysters."

"It sounds...basic." It sounded positively primitive.

"Basic," he repeated thoughtfully. "Yeah, I guess you could call it that. Traditionally, an island man built his own house and his own boat, tied his nets and managed to get enough fish and fowl to trade for staples over across the sound."

"And the women? Traditionally speaking, that is." Delle toyed with her milky glass. She hadn't drunk milk in years.

"Oh, they helped. Raised the babies, plucked the fowl, corned the fish, cooked the collards. Some tied and mended nets, and a few even helped fish them."

"Sounds like a rugged life." But then, he was a rugged man. It occurred to Delle that there was something oddly appealing about such a straightforward approach to life. No games, no role-playing. A woman would know exactly where she stood with such a man.

"Evidently it had its rewards. Enough of them stuck it out through the years. Fishermen are a pretty independent breed, all things considered. No subsidies, no guaranteed price support and no government agencies to pay a man for not fishing his nets." His grin was as charming as it was unexpected. "Always plenty of red tape and regulations, though."

It was not only his words that Delle found so fascinating, it was the expression on his mobile features. Cheekbones that were high and pronounced, lean cheeks sweeping down to a strong jaw and a determined chin. Most remarkable of all were his eyes. The light of laughter never seemed to be far from the surface, and yet there were depths there, too. Depths that were alive with meaning, with feeling.

She was being ridiculously fanciful, Delle chided herself.

Still, she had to admit that there was an element about this man that set him apart from all the other men she'd ever met, and it had nothing to do with the obvious differences in their backgrounds.

"Am I boring you?" The words broke softly into her troublesome thoughts.

"Oh, no—please go on with what you were saying," she said quickly, embarrassed to have been caught daydreaming. "It's fascinating!"

"Fascinating? The price of fish?"

"Yes, well…commerce. It's an interesting subject," Delle muttered in an effort to recover.

Crow's-feet deepened at the corners of his eyes as Cyrus teased her gently. "Yes, isn't it? As I was saying, the price of fish is regulated by the laws of supply and demand. When the fish aren't there, the price is pie-in-the-sky."

Delle focused her attention on his mouth, determined not to be caught drifting again. She liked the shape of his mouth. It was generous without being soft, firm without being hard. She liked his voice. There was just a hint of the island brogue she'd noticed in Lavada, making it difficult to evaluate his background.

"A man dreams of making that one big haul and paying off his bills. Gill netting, pound netting, beach hauling, long hauling or trawling—it's hard work with no guarantees. He might catch a thousand boxes, he might not get anything. If he strikes it lucky, chances are by the time he gets his catch to market, the price has already started dropping. The next day, it might be so low it wouldn't pay his fuel costs to go out."

The lips stopped moving. He was obviously waiting for her to make some intelligent comment, and she struggled to think of one. "Then why doesn't he get smart and move away, find a job that will provide a steady paycheck?"

Cyrus shrugged. "Some do. Most come back again, eventually."

"To starve?" she scoffed, not understanding such a lack of ambition.

"I doubt that many of them starve. As for those that stick it out, they might lose a few sets of nets, might even lose more than that, but the important thing is, they know who they are and what they want out of life."

"That's something, at least," Delle admitted. She could identify with the sentiment, if not the goal.

"It's everything," Cyrus said quietly.

Delle continued to stare at him, taking in the network of fine lines that fanned out at the corners of his eyes, the sun-streaked layers of his hair. Why should a recital of one man's views on the economic facts of a fisherman's life set off such an unlikely response deep inside her? She dealt in such realities every day of her life.

Shocked at the urge she felt to place her hand in his and share something she couldn't even begin to understand, she forced herself to laugh. "Somehow, I pictured today's fishing boats as being filled with all sorts of electronic gear, fish-finding equipment and automatic gadgets. You make it sound as if they're a cross between the ark and *Kon-Tiki*."

"There are still plenty of men who get along with the basics—a set of nets and a means of getting out to where the fish are."

"And plenty who want more and aren't afraid to go after it," she countered.

Cyrus nodded thoughtfully, but remained silent. For some reason, his amenability was beginning to ruffle Delle's composure.

"They could always borrow for better equipment," she suggested.

"They could."

Was he baiting her? Delle attempted to analyze his brief response. Failing to find anything contentious, she examined his expression as if he were a client intent on making her tip her hand without tipping his own. It was a game she played well, usually.

"I wasn't suggesting they hold up an armored car, you know," she said dryly. "Banks are a vital link in the nation's economic chain. There's nothing shameful about borrowing money."

"You sound a bit defensive," Cyrus said. "Let me guess—your father is a banker, right?"

It was tempting. Oh, it was so tempting. He'd left himself wide open, and Delle could have annihilated him with a few well-chosen words, but it would have been too easy.

The man was an anachronism. No wonder he sounded like a relic from the great depression; he evidently hadn't set foot off this island in the past fifty years. What would he say if she told him that as vice president and corporate loan officer of a Tidewater bank, just last week she'd helped make it possible for a Norfolk fisherman to purchase nearly a million dollars' worth of oceangoing trawler? Of course, technically speaking, the loan was made to a conglomerate rather than to a single fisherman, but that was beside the point.

For a moment, Delle was tempted to shake him out of his state of male complacence, but then she relented. He was a nice anachronism. A stunningly attractive one, too, and she couldn't find it in her heart to tell him that she probably made more in a day than he earned in a week. "My father's in business. I'm the one who works in a bank," she told him.

"Nice work for a woman. Good hours, piped in music, indoor plumbing and everything, huh?"

In the process of scratching a bite on her forehead, Delle paused. It occurred to her that she'd been itching—and scratching—all evening. Ever since her aborted bath, in fact. "Don't spread it on too thick, Cyrus. Incidentally, your friend at the store mentioned baking soda for my bites, but I forgot to get it. Know any other good home remedies?"

"Sorry, I don't get bitten, so I've never had to worry about it. Have you checked to see if there's any soda here?"

"Even if there was, it's supposed to go in a bath and I've already had my quota." She found herself telling him about the trouble with the drain and the limited supply of hot water. It was surprisingly pleasant to talk to a man when there wasn't the matter of a few million dollars riding on the conversation. Even a man whose ideas on women's role in society were more archaic than her father's.

"Why don't I have a look at the drain right now? Probably just came unhooked."

Cyrus led the way to the bathroom as if he were familiar with the layout of the house. It occurred to Delle that he probably was. How many handymen could an island the size of Coranoke support?

Five minutes later, the drain was working perfectly, and he said something about getting his meter and checking the hot water heater.

"I'd appreciate it. When my friends get back, we might have a problem."

"They're coming back?"

"Of course they're coming back. June—Mrs. Gavin, that is, had an impacted wisdom tooth. They took her back to civilization to see a dentist."

She didn't miss the tightening of his lips at the implied slight, and she regretted the slip. After all, he could no more help his background than she could hers. "Well, you *don't* have a dentist here, do you?" she said defensively.

"Not that I know of."

"All right, then," she said shortly. Tactlessness was not usually one of her failings. She'd been taught at an early age that courtesy was obligatory, especially to people in a less advantaged position. "I think Hetty mentioned knowing a dentist in Kitty Hawk, but they must have had trouble getting an appointment. I'm expecting them most any time now."

"I'll see what I can do about your hot water. If I have to order a new element, it could take a while. In which case, you'll either have to heat water on the stove or take cold showers."

"I could always move into a hotel for a few days, but as it happens, I'm used to cold showers."

The dancing light returned to his eyes, making her aware that she'd missed it for a few moments. "That bad, huh?"

"In the mornings. *To wake myself up*," she added repressively. "But I need a hot soak at night to help me sleep."

One dark eyebrow quirked in sympathy. "Have you tried warm milk?"

"To bathe in?"

"To drink."

"I think I'd rather bathe in it," she said with a shudder.

"It's not bad at all with a dash of rum or brandy."

"Unfortunately, I have neither."

"I'll bring you something when I get my meter."

"If you'll just go get your meter and fix my hot water, I won't need it," she reasoned.

Whatever his reply might have been, it was cut off by the phone. "That has to be the gulls," Delle muttered, hurrying to answer it. "It's about time."

Five minutes later she flopped on the couch, crossed her arms over her chest and stared at a deep gouge on the hatch-cover coffee table. "Nuts!"

"Anything wrong?" Cyrus spoke from the bathroom door. He'd evidently heard the whole conversation, as the cottage was too small to provide much in the way of privacy.

"They've canceled."

"Who's canceled what?"

"The gulls have canceled the T-Potty."

Tilting his shaggy head, he considered her thoughtfully. "Does the Audubon Society know about this?"

"What?" Distractedly, she scratched the right side of her jaw and then a place on the back of her neck. At this rate she'd look like Lazarus by the time her stay here was over. Which might be tomorrow—or even today.

"The things with the gulls," Cyrus prompted.

Delle attempted a laugh that fell short of the mark. She was absurdly disappointed. In spite of all its shortcomings, in spite of what she'd implied about the lack of civilization, she was beginning to grow rather fond of this rugged little sandbar. It was restful, if nothing else.

"The Gulls' T-Potty—it's sort of an annual reunion," she explained listlessly. "We were together eight years, first at the academy and then at college. Hetty and I started out as roommates, and since Paula and June came from Hetty's hometown, we sort of migrated together and stuck. In the tenth grade, we had this housemother who was determined to civilize us. Every *Thu'sday* afternoon, her *gu'ls* had to dress up and sip lukewarm tea and nibble stale cookies for thirty minutes. By the clock. It was compulsory." She could laugh about it now, but it had been agony at fifteen.

"And did she? Civilize you, that is?"

That grin again. Delle answered it with a reluctant smile of her own. "Not noticeably," she admitted, and decided on the spot that it had been worth coming down here just to meet this extraordinary man. When things got deadly tedious back at the bank, she could always daydream.

She might as well; she hadn't left room in her schedule for much else for the next ten or fifteen years. "We managed to get through the academy without being expelled for behavior unbecoming a lady, but it was touch and go for a while." Leaning back, she rested her hands palm up on the sofa beside her and lifted her bare feet—bare, that was, except for a matched pair of adhesive bandages on her little toes—to the scarred coffee table. "Lord, I'm tired. I was just beginning to get into the spirit of this place, and now this."

"Was it the wisdom tooth?" Cyrus relaxed into the chair across from her. It occurred to Delle that if a man in his position had flopped down on her white tweed sofa and made himself at home after fixing a leaky drain, she'd have hustled him out of there, pronto. Did that mean she was a snob? Or did it simply mean that Cyrus Burrus was a special type of man?

A little of both, she decided, sighing heavily. "It's not the tooth, the tooth's just fine. It's the forecast. Rain, rain and more rain. They've decided to cut their losses and go on back home."

"Reckon the folks around here are going to have to take a hint from our neighbors three states south and start calling it liquid sunshine." His eyes sparkled with laughter under a pair of somber brows. "We're still a little naive in some respects."

"It's no joke, darn it. This was supposed to be my vacation."

"Coranoke's not a bad place to sit out the rainy season. Whole different landscape, different feeling. Restful. That's what vacations are all about, isn't it?"

He couldn't be as guileless as he looked. All the same, he'd made one good point. Most years she managed to squeeze in a couple of days with the gulls. Other than that, last year she'd crammed a few hours of skiing into a national banking group conference and called it a vacation. The year before, she'd toured thirteen financial houses in Europe on a sort of busman's holiday. She'd come back from both trips exhausted. "Restful, hmm. Maybe you're right. Lately my vacations have been anything but that."

Come to think of it, these get-togethers with the gulls weren't all that restful, either. She loved her friends, but somehow, after one of their reunions, she always seemed to come away with vague feelings of dissatisfaction. The pressure at work always seemed fiercer than ever after a hiatus—the pressure of trying to hold her own in the constant power struggle, the fear of making a bad loan, or of missing out on one she should have had in the bag.

It happened, too, in spite of all she could do. Delle lived in dread of a repeat of her first transaction as a corporate loan officer. One million dollars at stake, and the director of finance of an important foundry had taken offense at something she'd said in all innocence. He'd given her competitor the nod, and she'd been out in the cold, after weeks of work. She'd gone through hell for weeks afterwards, waking up night after night in a cold sweat.

Heavens, the last thing she needed was pressure on her vacation!

Cyrus's gaze continued to rest lightly on her face. There was nothing at all demanding about the look he gave her, yet Delle was aware of a subtle pressure of another sort. She shifted position on the couch, and one hand moved to her hair in an uncharacteristic gesture of insecurity.

"So why not stay on?" he asked after a few moments.

"I'm tempted. There's just one hitch. Hetty hinted that they'd fixed me up with another man, and they might not be able to change the plans." At Cyrus's look of amused disbelief, Delle found herself describing some of the past attempts to fix her up with a male companion. "Nothing I can say seems to make a dent," she added helplessly. "Why is it that all happily married women are so hell-bent on marrying off every single man or woman in the world? These women are supposed to be my best friends. They know my plans for the future, and still they're determined to throw every stumbling block they can find in my path."

"You're not interested in stumbling blocks of a masculine nature?"

"Absolutely not. At least not of a matrimonial nature. I have my plans all mapped out, and there's no room for detours or distractions along the way. They know that."

"A man might be tempted to take that as a challenge," Cyrus observed mildly.

Delle sent him a withering look. "Are you speaking rhetorically? I assure you I don't mean it as a challenge."

"No, I didn't really think you did," he replied, and she examined his words suspiciously. "I expect your friends are just concerned about you." He leaned back in his chair, extending his crossed legs out before him, and Delle found herself heartily wishing he'd go home and put on more clothes. She'd never thought much about it before, but it seemed she was turning into a leg woman. Not to mention a shoulder woman. There was also that chest of his....

Heaven help her, she was coming down with mildew of the brain! Jerking her eyes away, she glared at the rain that cascaded down the northeast-facing windows. "All right, so they're concerned. Does that give them the right to interfere? Do I try to lure them away from their Little League and their PTA to sell real estate or design computers? I would never be so presumptuous."

Cyrus pursed his lips, and Delle wondered if she was becoming a mouth woman, too. The truth was that everything about the man appealed to her. Purely in an abstract way, that is. She tried to rationalize on the grounds that she

was on vacation, and therefore her mind wasn't functioning at peak efficiency, but it was a weak defense. The man
was unique. He was totally outside her limited experience,
and she retained just enough objectivity to be amazed at her
own reactions.

A bank officer and a handyman? There was simply no
meeting ground. Her errant imagination dredged up half-
remembered scenes from *Lady Chatterley's Lover*, and a
wash of color swept up her throat and burned her cheeks.

"Sounds like you're a dedicated career woman."

"Is there any other kind? A *job* might not require dedi-
cation, a career does, if you want to succeed."

"You do, of course."

"Certainly I do," Delle snapped. This was ludicrous.
Why should she sit here calmly discussing her personal life
with this half-naked native when she ought to be packing?
This would give her a few more days to look around New
York and decide if she really wanted to move north. There
was always Atlanta.

"I happen to be very good at what I do," she declared,
jumping up to dig through her purse and pull out a fresh roll
of antacid tablets. She popped two into her mouth and
scowled at the unremitting rain that turned the landscape
into a hazy monochrome. "Look, I've got to start getting
ready to leave if I want to catch that last ferry."

"Headache? Let me get you some water to take those
with."

"No! I mean I don't need anything. They're not aspirin."

"Oh." Without moving a muscle, Cyrus continued to
study her, and Delle shook her head.

"Cyrus, I'm sorry. I didn't mean to snap at you. It's my
stomach."

"The fish?"

"No, it's just . . ." Sighing, she returned to the couch and sank down. "I think I must be on the verge of an ulcer." Not even to Daniel had she confided her fear. He'd have railroaded her into going for all sorts of horrid tests.

"Then I can't think of anything more helpful than a few days of lazing around here. No pressure, no commitments, no reason to do anything you don't feel like doing. You can even unplug the phone if you want to, then nothing can bother you."

"Want to bet?" she retorted dryly. Offhand, she could think of several things that could bother her, and she wasn't referring to the mosquitoes.

He shrugged. "Worth a try."

Delle admitted to herself that the idea held a certain appeal. A few days of no pressure and no commitments before she tackled New York would be the best medicine she could take. It might take a bit of getting used to, but she was in the mood to try.

"What if this man they've sent me turns up on my doorstep?"

"You can always refuse delivery, can't you?" A shadow of suspicion rose up in Cyrus's mind, but he quickly dismissed it. Just because they were from Charlotte—just because he and Gavin had had offices in the same building . . .

Delle shook her head. "It's just so awkward. The poor fellow is as much a victim as I am, you know. It's hardly his fault my three best friends happen to be harpies who prey on the flesh of single men. Honestly, Cyrus, it gets to be embarrassing after a while."

"Not to mention dangerous. You're all alone here," Cyrus reminded her.

"It's having some strange man hanging over my head that bothers me, not any possible danger. A man who lets himself be manipulated by those three can't be much of a threat. Anyway, I can take care of myself."

"All the same—"

Delle cut him short. "Look, I can manage a simple brush-off. I'm an expert, if you want to know the truth."

"I'll just bet you are," he drawled with a look that she'd like to think was admiration. It probably wasn't. "Well, remember, I'm usually within shouting distance."

"Thanks," she said ungraciously.

"Just thought I'd offer. Meanwhile, if you get to feeling like company, I might start taking down some of that paneling. Notice the brown fungus sprouting between the boards over near the corner?" He hauled in his legs and stood, flexing his shoulders without making a production of it.

Yes, Delle decided, she was definitely a shoulder woman. Her fingers curled as she tried to imagine what it would feel like to touch the hard muscles under the soft navy sweatshirt. "Fungus," she repeated absently. *"Fungus?"*

"Won't hurt a thing, but it means I'd better work on that flashing as soon as the weather clears. Meanwhile, let me know when you're going to be out, and I'll get started in here."

Delle gave up. There were reasons pro and con both going and staying, but at the moment she was simply too tired to make the decision. She'd go with the line of least resistance, and as she was already there, that meant she'd stay a while longer.

She yawned, apologized and then did it again.

"Why not go back to bed?" Cyrus suggested.

Evidently she'd used her small store of energy on the decision to stay, because the idea was irresistible. "Actually, I could do with a nap. Some heartless creature woke me before daylight this morning by pounding on the roof right over my bed. I thought the sky was falling."

"It is, but it won't last forever. Just a little liquid sunshine, remember?"

"Don't give me that chamber of commerce line or I might feel compelled to go out and do something touristy, and at the moment, I'm too sleepy."

"Now you're getting into the spirit. My grandmother had a theory about rainy days. She claimed that since housewives worked seven days a week, and twice as hard on holidays, rainy days were a gift from God. Whenever it rained, she did the bare minimum and spent the rest of her time reading, napping and playing dominoes. Wouldn't allow herself to do laundry or cleaning, no matter how long it rained. Grannie claimed that by the time the sun came out again, she was so full of energy she could last out a Sahara-size drought."

Delle slept for hours and awoke just before dark, starving again. At this rate, she'd be splitting the seams of her new gray pin-striped suit. She got dressed again and drove to the store, where she stocked up on canned goods and crackers.

"Might be stale," Lavada warned. "Hard to keep 'em crisp in all this dampness."

"At this point, I'm too hungry to be critical. Mrs. Scarborough, do you have any baking soda? I've scratched myself raw."

"You can call me Lavada," the large, gray-haired woman offered with a singularly sweet smile.

Delle responded in kind. "Thanks. I'm Cordelia Richardson—Delle to my friends."

Back at the cottage, she opened a can of vegetable soup, dumped it into a pan and heated it. That much she could do, at least. It didn't look exactly right—perhaps it was old. There was such a thing as shelf life, wasn't there? Even for canned goods? She poked at the lumpy mess for a few moments, and after a few bites, decided she wasn't quite so hungry after all.

Idly, she wondered where Cyrus was and what he was doing. Perhaps she'd misunderstood him when he said he'd be back with whatever it took to fix her hot water heater.

The water heater managed to supply her with enough lukewarm water for a hip-deep soak, and she dumped in a handful of baking soda and hoped for the best. She'd hate to stroll into Hanover Manufacturers' Trust for an appointment looking as if she had smallpox.

By nine, Delle was asleep again, and for reasons she was at a loss to explain, slept better than she had in years, waking refreshed and hungry shortly after dawn.

Cyrus let himself in the back door while she was trying to decipher the instructions on the coffee maker. Did he have the run of all the cottages on the island, or only hers?

"Morning," he greeted her cheerfully. "How're the bites?"

"Better. I got some soda from Lavada. I still itch a little, but at least I'm not so lumpy. You wouldn't happen to know how to make coffee in this contraption, would you? Mine's a different make."

He took the glass container from her hands, filled it under the faucet and spooned several measures of coffee into the filter. "Had breakfast yet?"

"I was trying to figure out how to make it. That sounds wonderful," she said a few moments later as the first gurgling stream began to filter down.

"I mean something to eat. You did say you were having stomach problems, didn't you?" He glanced at the cable-knit sweater that covered her flat abdomen and outlined her high breasts.

"I never have anything but coffee for breakfast."

"Worst thing you can do to your system. No wonder you've got trouble."

"Oh, so now you're a doctor as well as a carpenter and a fisherman? Part of that tradition of self-reliance, I suppose." Delle regretted her sarcasm. She tendered an apology, but Cyrus brushed it aside.

He went on calmly opening and closing cabinets, turning finally to the refrigerator to frown at its barren shelves. "What do your friends expect you to live on, salad dressing?"

"We'd have bought fish. Hetty likes to do things to seafood."

"I don't see the cream."

"I take my coffee black."

"Not with ulcers, you don't. You shouldn't be drinking it at all, but then you'd probably get caffeine withdrawal symptoms."

Delle sat down heavily in one of the sturdy ladder-back chairs. "You're one of the bossiest men I've ever met, do you know that? Tell me, where do you come by this all-encompassing wisdom of yours?"

"Believe it or not, you career ladies don't have a corner on ulcers."

"Career ladies! You make it sound like little girls playing dress-up. I happen to be a vice president of one of the largest banks in the commonwealth of Virginia, and in case you weren't aware of what goes on in the outside world, banks are those institutions that make all the wheels go around." She crossed her arms on the table, scowling at his broad back as he reached down two coffee cups.

"Milk'll do, I suppose." Calmly, Cyrus proceeded to pour the rest of the milk he'd brought with him the night before into a small pan. "Since you'll be drinking yours about half and half, I'd better heat it first."

"I'll drink mine—"

"The way I fix it," he finished evenly, switching on the front burner as the last of the coffee filtered through. It smelled heavenly, and Delle's stomach growled in response;

otherwise she'd probably have chased him out the back door.

"You'll burn in hell for this, you know that, don't you?"

"But your stomach won't," he said with a smile that only added to her frustration. "No eggs, no cereal here. Reckon milk toast made with crackers will have to do. There's just about enough milk left for one serving."

While she watched, amazed at the panache of this unlikely jack-of-all-trades, he buttered several crackers, sprinkled them lightly with sugar and placed them in a bowl. By then the milk was steaming, and he poured half in one cup and the rest over the crackers.

"If you think I'm going to eat that disgusting-looking mess, you're out of your mind."

He placed the bowl before her and handed her a spoon. "Want your coffee? Eat your milk toast first and you can have it."

"What is it with you primitive types? Do you get your kicks from torturing women?" She shoved the bowl across the table and reached for the coffeepot, but Cyrus caught her hand and began to stroke it.

"Temper, temper," he scolded gently. "You're probably pumping acid by the gallon. Is it worth it, just to score off my hide? I promise you, nothing you can say is going to make a dent in it. If our kamikaze mosquitoes can't get through, your pretty little claws aren't going to do much damage."

"Give me my coffee, Cyrus," Delle said through clenched teeth.

With one surprisingly well-shaped forefinger, he traced the veins that were beginning to show on the back of her clenched fist. "I'm trying to be your friend, Delle."

"I don't need a friend," she snarled. "I need my coffee!" To her acute dismay, she felt the familiar prickle begin at the backs of her eyes.

Not now, she thought helplessly, fighting back the irrational tears. *Oh, God, that's all I need to make my day complete!*

Four

Eat half of it," Cyrus compromised. He pulled up a chair beside her and placed the bowl in front of her again, and in a gesture of surrender, Delle lifted her spoon.

"I abhor soggy food," she grumbled, blinking hard to conquer the crazy threat of tears. Perhaps she should have let them flow; then maybe he'd have been embarrassed enough to leave her alone. Men hated tears. Except for this recent aberration, she hadn't cried for years.

"Go on, taste it," Cyrus urged. "It'll act as a buffer for the coffee." He was so close she could feel the heat from his body, smell the scent of soap and toothpaste, and something subtly masculine. Something untamed.

Untamed? The thought came out of the blue. It slipped away almost before it registered, and Delle said, "Caffeine has never bothered me." She tasted the stuff. It wasn't good, but it wasn't exactly awful.

Cyrus was all quiet solicitude. "It's not the caffeine, it's the acid. Coffee and alcohol are about the two worst offenders in a case like this."

She forced down another spoonful. "You sound as if you've been there."

He merely shrugged, and Delle found herself wondering why such an obviously capable and attractive man had chosen to bury himself in such a place. Eyeing the coffeepot longingly, she spooned up another sodden cracker and tried to pretend it was a new and different dessert. Perhaps he was afraid to tackle the mainland, afraid of failure. He was obviously an intelligent man, even a sensitive one.

Moved by an uncomfortable mixture of irritation and empathy, she said, "Look, I know how important it is to feel as if you're in control of your life, Cyrus. I'm that way, too, you know. I pride myself on being self-sufficient. A place like Coranoke—well, different frogs require different size ponds." God, how smug she sounded! She'd meant to be reassuring, not patronizing. "What I mean is—"

"I think I know what you mean," Cyrus said calmly, looking as if he could have easily handled a pond the size of the Atlantic.

Delle sighed. So much for tact and diplomacy.

"All finished? I'll wash up while you have your coffee."

Didn't he have a single word to say in his own defense? Didn't he realize that a man of his obvious intelligence and abilities was wasted down here on this forsaken scrap of land? "There's no dishwasher, you know," she informed him out of sheer frustration.

"Aw, jeez! I guess I'll just have to throw 'em away." But he was already at the sink, the sleeves of his faded sweatshirt shoved up to reveal powerful, golden-furred forearms. A teasing smile played hide-and-seek at the corners of his mouth, and Delle's lips tightened.

She shook her head, sipping the diluted coffee as she gazed in frustration at his powerful back. Why waste time worrying about the tender sensibilities of a man she'd never see again? "My own self-sufficiency includes being able to hire a housekeeper," she said, still conscious of an obscure need to defend herself. "Actually, I've never been very domestic." In her father's well-staffed house, it hadn't been possible. Since then she'd had neither the time nor the energy.

"Bachelors sometimes have to be."

"Working women sometimes do, too, but fortunately, I can afford to concentrate on—other things." *Other* things, not *more important* things. She was learning. Finishing her coffee, she leaned back, rather surprised to discover that she felt fine. As a rule, her stomach was in an uproar by this time of the morning. Could a simple thing like breakfast have made such a difference?

"Any plans for the day?" Cyrus, a pink-striped dish towel draped over his shoulder, turned to confront her.

"Nothing in particular. Why, do you want to look at the hot water heater or start tearing down walls?"

A blob of suds clinging to one elbow, he leaned his hips against the edge of the sink and studied the woman before him. Tearing down walls? The more he saw of her, the more he'd like to tear down that thick one she'd built up around herself, if only to see what was behind it. As to what came after that, he wouldn't even venture a guess. She really wasn't the sort of woman he could afford to get interested in. A summer woman, possibly? No. Definitely not a summer woman.

"I came back by here yesterday afternoon," he explained, "But you were sacked out and I didn't have the heart to start beating on the plumbing."

"You came inside?" She frowned, conscious of a tingling sensation in the pit of her stomach that had nothing to do with digestive problems. "You came inside while I was asleep?" God, that was even worse than his coming inside while she was gone.

"Sorry." The word was a simple apology, the expression in his eyes something rather more complex. "I knocked, but you didn't answer. I thought maybe you'd gone exploring again. I left as soon as I saw you asleep on the couch."

She should have gone to bed and locked the bedroom door. It simply hadn't occurred to her that anyone would barge in unannounced that way. "You don't believe in standing on ceremony, do you?"

"I don't mean to make a nuisance of myself."

Delle stared at him in dismay. How did one deal with such a man? The rules that applied in her portion of the world didn't seem to exist on this tiny, out-of-the-way sandbar. At least, not to a man like Cyrus.

Strangely enough, she wasn't at all certain she wanted them to.

"The drum are running." Cyrus offered the information in an offhand manner, his face turned away so that she couldn't see the expression in his eyes. "Care to try your luck?"

"What is it, some kind of a marching band?"

"Drum fish."

Delle frowned. The man had invaded her privacy. Deliberately or not, he was undermining her peace of mind. "If you mean do I want to go fishing, I don't think so, Cyrus. I don't know the first thing about it, and I don't have any equipment."

"I've got all the equipment you need, I know how to use it and I'm ready and willing to teach you everything I know."

Delle watched, fascinated, as his lips framed the last word. His upper lip was sharply chiseled, his lower one firm and full. What would that mouth feel like against hers? Warm, moist, moving...

"Look, Delle, no matter how tired you feel, it's just not good to sleep too much. A thrill a day keeps the doctor away—at least it keeps your circulation going."

If that were true, Delle thought wryly, she could just imagine the Guiness Book of Records recording the fact that a certain mythical Mrs. Cyrus Burrus, at age ninety-nine, was discovered to have the circulation of a sixteen-year-old girl.

Cyrus's gaze seemed to bore its way right through to her deepest thoughts, and to her chagrin, Delle felt the heat rise to her face. Twice in less than an hour the man had brought a rush of color to her cheeks. What was happening to her? Why would a woman who had only played about in the shallows when it came to the physical side of romance begin turning perfectly innocent remarks into double entendres?

"Fishing," she mumbled a little desperately. She'd better go for it on the off chance that the effect he had on her would be diluted by fresh air. "But you may as well know that I've never even held a rod in my hands."

"No problem. A little hands-on demonstration will have you swinging like a pro. Believe me, you'll wonder why you waited so long."

Delle shook her head in an effort to clear it. She'd been working too hard. She'd waited too long to take a vacation. Daniel had said she was headed for a breakdown if she didn't ease off. Her father had said—

Never *mind* what her father had said. She no longer ran her life according to her father's precepts. Taking a firm grip on herself, she declared, "I'd love to go fishing with you, Cyrus. Do I need to wear anything special or am I all right?"

His eyes skimmed over her in swift appraisal, making her acutely conscious of the low V of her sweater, the way the loose knit clung to her breasts before snuggling about her hips. Here I go again, she agonized. There was nothing even faintly revealing about a heavy, hand knit pullover and a pair of tailored slacks, so why did she feel as if his eyes had blazed a trail down her naked body?

"I don't suppose you have a sou'wester?"

"A raincoat? You mean we're going now? In the rain?"

"It's beginning to slack off. By the time I collect my gear, it'll be just heavy mist."

"Then why would I need a raincoat?"

"The wind off the water's damp. It can chill you even when it's not all that cold. Never mind, I'll bring along something for you to wear."

Cyrus finished the dishes and moved toward the back door, and Delle followed, oddly reluctant to see him leave. What if he changed his mind and didn't come back? Now that she'd made up her mind to go along with him, the thought of hanging around all day alone with nothing to do lost much of its appeal. "How about boots? I didn't bring my boots, either."

"The water's still pretty warm, considering it's November. Matter of fact, that's why the big ones aren't in yet, but they've been catching a few yearling drum on the north beach at Hatteras. Let's see if this wind shift brought a few of them on down here."

Delle's gaze followed him until he disappeared into the woods. Strange man, she mused. Not at all the sort of man one would expect to discover here on the Outer Banks. Or perhaps, she corrected, he was precisely the sort of man one could expect to find on a narrow chain of islands that had been settled a few years after the first English explorers had come to this country, and then largely isolated until the middle of the twentieth century.

Goodness knows, if rugged independence was a requirement, Cyrus qualified. As for that indefinable magnetism he seemed to radiate, that was probably nothing more than her imagination. Or simple biology. She'd been too busy to worry about biology for years, but evidently it was still alive and well. She'd have to watch it.

Some twenty minutes later, Cyrus pulled up in the driveway. Three surf rods rose high above the Blazer's rusted hood from the bumper-mounted holders. The space in back was cluttered with a bait bucket, a large tackle box, a shovel, a tire pump and a battered-looking ice chest.

He tossed her a lined, windproof jacket. "Here, try this on. It'll swallow you, but as long as your body's warm, your feet aren't apt to freeze." Delle slid her arms into the sleeves, laughing when only her fingertips emerged from the cuffs. Grinning, Cyrus captured her hand and rolled back each cuff. "Alterations done on the spot," he quipped.

Was she being fanciful or had something kindled in his eyes when he held her hand for a moment? Delle's skin tingled from his touch long after he released her fingers.

They pulled out of her driveway and headed for the beach, and she felt her nerves tighten still further with excitement. Happy excitement. It was distinctly different from the sort of sick tension she so often felt at work, or before one of the infrequent dinners with her father.

Cyrus was whistling something vaguely familiar under his breath. Oddly enough, the fact that he couldn't carry a tune didn't bother her in the least, despite the fact that she'd been practically born with life memberships in the civic opera society and the symphony series.

Perched on the edge of the passenger seat, her hands clasped in her lap, Delle peered through the pitted, salt-hazed windshield at a streak of pale blue in the sky. "How did you know the rain was nearly over? More island lore?"

Cyrus nodded gravely. "Part of the island tradition. Always tune in the weather report before you offer to take a lady to the beach."

Delle was still grinning when they passed one of the fishermen she'd seen the day before. He was still working on his nets. When Cyrus lifted a finger in greeting, the man responded in like manner.

"Not exactly chatty, is he? He looked at me yesterday as if I were an escaped convict or something."

"Cromer's just shy. Once you get to know him, he'll open up. Always did have an eye for a good-looking woman."

"Yes, well... as far as I'm concerned, he can stick to his crocheting. I'd rather take my chances with whatever Hetty sent me. I tend to lose patience with the strong, silent type."

"Remind me to keep talking."

"Feel free to sing instead," Delle said magnanimously.

"Can't carry a tune."

"I noticed."

Cyrus pinched her thigh gently and then concentrated on downshifting to negotiate the sandy turnoff that led to the beach.

"This is fun. You know, I feel almost like a kid setting off for summer camp," Delle confided as they skirted a large puddle of water that stretched across the road.

He spared her a quizzical look. "You must lead a deprived life."

"Just because I've never been fishing? That doesn't—" They were nearing the end of the unpaved road, and suddenly she clutched his arm. "Stop!"

Cyrus braked, and Delle slid down from the high seat and darted across to the edge of the bushes. A moment later, she returned. "I told you so!" she cried triumphantly, holding up an empty bottle and a pair of ruined sandals.

Cyrus's laughter was deep and wholehearted, and after a moment she joined in, tossing the relics into the back along with the assortment of fishing gear. "I told you I'd recognize that bush again, and I did. It looks different when you're coming from the other direction."

"A few strips of soggy leather and a no-return bottle. Was it worth it?"

"It's the principle of the thing," she said smugly, laughter still lurking in her dark eyes.

"Yeah," Cyrus scoffed. Shifting into low again, he set off toward the beach, disdaining the many tracks in evidence to create one of his own.

There were half a dozen fishermen strung out along the shoreline, but Cyrus turned in the opposite direction and drove for several minutes, scanning the surf. Delle watched him, admiring the easy way he handled the sharp hillocks called camelbacks and the frequent patches of soft sand left by the ebbing tide. Beach driving couldn't be all that easy, even with four-wheel drive, but he managed to make it seem as effortless as tooling a powerful luxury car along an open stretch of highway.

"There they are," he murmured, pulling up to a higher level before cutting the engine.

"The fish? Are you telling me you can actually see them?"

"Not yet, but I can smell 'em. Do you mean to tell me you *can't*?" He sent her a look of teasing disbelief.

"I don't see or smell anything but ocean, and frankly, I don't believe you do either." From the passenger seat, Delle leaned forward to see around him. Was there a fishy smell? There was certainly nothing fishy to see.

"Hop down and come around here and I'll show you." Cyrus continued to study the surf, and unconvinced, Delle dropped to the sand and strolled around to the other side of the rusty beach buggy. The moment she came within range of Cyrus's arm, he corralled her, pulling her back against his chest, and Delle, suddenly aware of a constriction in her own chest, found herself pinned between his knees. Still seated in the driver's seat, facing the turgid surf, he leaned over until his head was level with hers. Resting one arm over her shoulder, he pointed seaward. "There, see those breakers rolling in over the sandbar? See the smooth place where they're not breaking? That's a slough. It's where the bait fish hang out, and that's where we're going to catch our dinner."

"Our dinner?"

"What were you expecting, a trophy to hang on your office wall?"

She hadn't been expecting anything, as a matter of fact, but now that he mentioned it, maybe she should try for something to compete with the royal blue and silver marlin that hung over the senior vice president's desk. Harry tailored his fish stories to suit his client, but Delle had a sneaking suspicion that the monstrous thing hanging there had been ordered from an office supplies catalog.

"I'm not sure I even know what a drum fish looks like."

"This time of year you can usually see plenty of mug shots in the sports pages."

"I don't read the sports pages. It's all I can do to get through the financial page, the front page and the editorial page."

"Not the comics?"

Delle's lips twitched. She was acutely aware of the solid wall of his chest against her back, of the hand on her shoulder. She caught the scent of his skin and inhaled deeply. "I'm going to start saving those for rainy days."

"You do that," he said warmly. "Actually, you can see fish underwater more often than you might think. Blues, for instance, will slash back and forth through a school of bait fish until it looks like someone's firing buckshot into the water. The gulls clean up after them, so if you're after blues, you look for feeding gulls."

"I don't see a single gull." Was it her imagination, or did he lean closer? His warm breath moved through her hair like a current of tropical air, paralyzing her for a long moment.

"A school of drum, on the other hand, looks almost red when you see it under the right conditions," he continued.

Were they actually talking about fish? She could have sworn that they were talking about something altogether different.

"You might even mistake drum for a patch of seaweed floating just under the surface of the water. Actually they're channel bass, but they're called drum because they make a drumming sound—red drum because of the color. The last two world records were taken over on Hatteras Island. A ninety and a ninety-four pounder."

Delle pulled away and twisted around. "Cyrus, if you think I'm going to risk catching a hundred pounds of *any-thing*, you're crazy. You go ahead and fish all you want to, I'll collect shells, or—or watch for feeding reds. Or blues— or whatever." Was it her imagination, or was that a know-ing look in those wicked eyes of his? He couldn't possibly know how his touch had affected her.

Abruptly, she turned her back, taking a few deep breaths of the soft sea air to clear her brain. If Cyrus had suggested this outing to give her a little exercise, that was one thing. If the purpose had been relaxation, then they might as well forget it. Relaxation was the last thing she'd felt a moment ago when he was all but holding her in his arms.

"I brought along salt mullet and fatback heads," he said.

Salt mullet and fatback heads? Delle got a grip on her overworked imagination and peered into the bucket he slid across the tailgate. "You don't expect me to actually *touch* that mess, do you?"

Cyrus released a rig from one of the rods and proceeded to bait the hook with a silvery fish head. "Tide looks just about right, so we'll fish it on out and then halfway in again. Unless you get tired, that is."

"Tired? *Me?* I'm strong as a horse."

Cyrus's concern gave way to a guileless smile. "Great! As I was saying, I prefer the fish heads, but I thought you might like to try mullet."

She shot him a suspicious glance. "If you think I'm going to eat anything that would eat a fish head, you're crazy."

Wiping a sliver of sandpaper over the large hook dangling from the second rod, Cyrus reached for the bucket. "Why don't I go ahead and bait up for you this time? You can try whatever you prefer next time, okay?"

"Prefer? Cyrus, I wasn't kidding when I said I didn't know how to fish. I've figured out that the bait goes on one end and the fisherman on the other, but that's about all."

Wiping his hands on a stained scrap of towel, he said slowly, "You're serious, aren't you? I thought being from Norfolk, you'd at least have a speaking acquaintance with some form of the sport."

She rolled up the legs of her slacks and zipped the jacket Cyrus had provided. Not that it was cold, but the wind seemed to cut through to the bone. "I grew up in a suburb of Richmond. My father used to take my three brothers to Scotland to fish for salmon every year while I stayed with the housekeeper. I have a speaking acquaintance with smoked salmon, Dover sole, swordfish steaks and broiled lobster, but that doesn't mean I know how to catch them."

Why had she told him that? It sounded as if she were either bragging or making a play for sympathy. "Oh, give me the damned rod. If Oren can do it, I can do it," she grumbled, struggling to lift the oversize surf rod from the spike.

If anyone else had been witness to her blundering attempts to cast, she'd have died of embarrassment. Somehow with Cyrus it didn't seem to matter. Sooner than she

would have believed possible, she was laughing right along
with him, actually provoking opportunities for him to move
in behind her and demonstrate the proper way to hold, to
swing and to release.

"Is this what you meant by a hands-on demonstration?"
she said, laughing while he worked the barb from the tail of
her jacket. "I hope not all your students are so inept."

"I'll admit I've had better ones. Stand still, will you? This
coat of mine will smell like fish for a month." They were
both barefoot, standing in a warm, frothy surf, and when
the sand crumbled beneath her feet, Delle clutched at his
shoulder for support, laughing helplessly.

"Speaking of fish," she gasped, "I'm starved. I don't
suppose you brought anything to eat?" It occurred to her
that she could have done that much, at least. If she'd known
what to bring. She was beginning to feel more than a little
incompetent, and it wasn't a feeling she particularly enjoyed. Nor one she was accustomed to.

They ate thick cheese sandwiches supplied by Cyrus and
drank milk from pint cartons, and Delle didn't think she'd
ever had anything quite so delicious in her life. "What kind
of cheese is this, it's marvelous!"

"Plain old generic brand cheddar." Cyrus grinned, enjoying her enjoyment. He checked to be sure the ratchet was
set on his reel and stretched out on the tarp he'd spread over
the damp sand, deliberately allowing his thoughts to scatter
at random.

There was a time when he'd put a lot of stock in serving a
perfectly ripened Brie. What a jerk he'd been. And all to
impress a woman who wasn't worth the effort. These past
few years had been the best of his whole life. He'd like to
think that generations of Burrus ancestors who'd called
these islands home for some three hundred years wouldn't
be embarrassed by his presence among them now.

Sitting close beside the sand spike that held her rod, Delle kept an intent eye on the arc of the line that disappeared beneath the surface a short distance offshore. She was wet to the hips and cold, but having too wonderful a time to admit it. "I'm still hungry," she said, startled to realize that it was true. "What else did you bring us?"

"You'll hold for a while." Cyrus laughed, leaning over to wipe the milk from the corners of her mouth. "The tide's just about perfect now, so we'd better get ready for action. Your line's washed in. Why don't you let me put it out for you?" Actually, it hadn't washed in all that much. She simply couldn't cast well enough yet to place it where it was supposed to be, in spite of the fact that she was wading out farther each time.

Delle scrambled to her feet, brushed the sand from her hands and snatched up her rod. "Put your own line out. I know where I want mine. See that little wavelet just to the right of the big one?"

Cyrus's face was solemn, his eyes dancing. "Why not wait until it comes ashore, make it easy for yourself?"

She made a face at him. "Go ahead and laugh, but I'm warning you—I have a reputation of getting what I go after, and I'm going after at least a thirty-pounder."

"Thirty, hmm? Somehow I figured you for a world record, at least."

"The male ego being such a delicate thing, I wouldn't dare, not my first time out." She reeled in, checked her bait, removed a few strands of eelgrass and, with both hands full of heavy rod, waded out hip deep into the surprisingly warm surf, ignoring his jeering response.

She'd be willing to bet that Cyrus had few problems with his ego on any count. She was fast coming to realize that behind that rough exterior of his lurked a pretty impressive individual.

Or perhaps she was assigning him qualities he didn't possess simply to justify her growing interest in him.

Placing her baited rig a little farther out than before, Delle backed ashore, a broad smile of sheer enjoyment on her face. She wouldn't catch a darned thing, but it really didn't matter, which was rather a surprising admission from someone who'd always been so highly competitive.

Correction: she hadn't always been competitive. In school, she'd been a washout as far as sports was concerned, because it simply hadn't mattered to her which group of girls won the day's game. She'd become a competent golfer out of determination, not competitiveness. There was a distinct difference.

Six years ago she'd stood quaking at the altar in her handmade-lace wedding dress and had made a public announcement that not only shocked the community but removed her permanently from the dubious shelter of her family and her home. Since that day, she hadn't dared look back.

It wasn't competitiveness that motivated her, Delle realized, it was sheer determination to make it on her own. One by one, she'd set up her goals and then gone about achieving them. After six years, she was well on her way to proving to her father and to Oren that—

"Hey, partner, want me to put it out for you? You'll never catch anything but seaweed where you are."

"Care to make a small wager?" she challenged. "Ten bucks says I'll catch the first fish." Well...maybe a *little* bit competitive.

Cyrus made a fine adjustment in the drag of his reel, checked the amount of line dangling from the tip and then grinned over his shoulder as he waded into the surf. "That's a bit rich for my blood, lady banker, but I'll think of something to make it interesting." With a movement as graceful as the flight of a heron, he whipped the limber rod through the air, hurling the ten-ounce weight directly to the middle of the narrow break in the sandbar.

Delle sighed with unconscious envy. After two hours of trying, she knew casting was more a matter of technique than of strength. Unfortunately, she had neither, but technique could be learned. Coranoke wasn't all that far from Norfolk, and judging by the way she felt now, surf fishing might be just what the doctor ordered for working off frustrations.

Suddenly, her rod was almost jerked from her hands. She gripped it tightly as the line screamed out, blundering in an effort to remember all she'd been told. "Cyrus, help me!" she yelled. "I've got a whale!"

"Hold your tip up!" Cyrus loped back up the beach to ram his own rod into a sand spike before hurrying to stand behind her. "You're doing fine," he said encouragingly as she struggled to keep from having her arms pulled from their sockets. "Just fine. Lift the tip, reel in and whatever you do, don't let him get any slack."

He stayed right behind her, coaching, instructing, and Delle grimaced as she struggled against the furiously determined creature on the other end of her line. She wasn't at all sure she could do it, but she certainly wasn't going to give in! Her arms were aching, her fingers were numb, and she found herself being drawn farther and farther out to sea. Everything she had on was wet and heavy, dragging her down as she struggled to land her catch.

"You're not going to get away from me, you lovely thing! Just wait until my father sees—" Her breath was coming in ragged gasps. "Stay still and let me reel you in, dammit!"

"He's getting tired," Cyrus said encouragingly from just over her shoulder.

"Who isn't?" Delle grunted. Hip deep in the surging water, she was leaning back against the drag and preparing to shift forward and reel in the slack when the tension suddenly snapped.

Delle stumbled backward. Cyrus managed to catch her, and they both floundered in the swift current and sat down hard. She hung on to the rod, unable to believe it was all over. "What happened?" she wailed. "Did I do it wrong?" A wave slapped her in the face, and then Cyrus was hauling her to her feet. The wind cut like ice through her drenched clothing as he pried the rod from her numb fingers and half carried her ashore.

"God, I ought to be horsewhipped," he muttered. "No experience, no rain gear, no waders, and I let you—"

"*Let* me!" Delle gasped. She was beginning to shake hard now, partly from cold, partly from the release of tortured muscles. "You didn't *let* me do anything, Cyrus. I'm responsible for my own actions, and don't you ever forget it." She turned away, a look of total defeat on her face. "I did it all wrong," she whispered.

Something inside Cyrus began to crumble, a protective crust that had formed around his innermost feelings a long time ago. It had gradually hardened over the years, and now he suddenly felt as vulnerable as a newly shed jimmy crab.

Placing one hand on her trembling shoulder, he turned her around and forced her to meet his eyes. "No, honey," he said firmly. "You did it all right. I'm the one who's at fault here, and I'd better start making up for it before you catch pneumonia." He plucked a strand of eelgrass from the side of her face, his hand lingering to cradle her trembling chin. "Some fishing guide I turned out to be. In every tug-of-war there is a winner and a loser. I guess this time, the fish was the winner. Come on, let's go build a fire and get you warm."

Five

Delle disappeared to run herself a hot bath while Cyrus built a fire in the fireplace. A few minutes after she'd settled into a scant ten inches of comfortably warm water, he called through the door.

"Did you have enough hot water?"

"Yes, but it was beginning to run tepid when I shut it off."

"I'll see about it," he promised. "Look, the fire's all set, the screen's in place and I'm going home to change. I'll be back by the time you're finished in there. Don't stay in long enough to get chilled."

Delle, her teeth still inclined to chatter, cast a derisive glance at the closed door. "Let me work my way through *thawing* before I start to worry about *chilling*, okay?"

She heard the soft sound of his laughter on the other side and sank deeper into the water. It was already beginning to cool off, and there was no more where that came from. On the point of asking him to heat her a kettleful, she heard the sound of the Blazer driving off.

Some thirty minutes later, the back door opened and slammed shut. Then came the clatter of pans in the kitchen. Half-dressed, Delle hurriedly pulled on a taupe cashmere turtleneck over her white flannels. She slathered moisturizer over her face and considered doing a complete job—shadow, mascara, blusher, the works. She decided against it. Her color was high enough as it was, thanks to the raw wind she'd been exposed to all morning.

Did windburn cause one's eyes to glitter this way? It must. Either that or she was feverish to the point of delirium.

She made several passes with the hair drier, fluffing with her fingers as she went, and left it at that. Her grooming wasn't up to standard, but then, what was? At least she no longer had seaweed and sand clinging to her body.

"Something smells marvelous!" she declared, strolling into the room where Cyrus was presiding over an enormous copper stock pot. "Great Scott, whose army are you feeding from that thing?"

"Go clear off a place on the coffee table. I'll be dishing it up as soon as I add the sherry."

Delle's gaze moved over his rugged frame, taking in the dry jeans, the red flannel shirt, the pink-striped towel tucked daintily under his belt. "Somehow, I always associated the song *Home on the Range* with bowlegged cowpokes in battered ten-gallon hats and flapping chaps. I never *dreamed....*" She looked pointedly at the towel at his waist and the soup pot on the built-in range.

With a low growl, Cyrus came at her, a cooking spoon in one tanned and callused hand. "Better watch your step or you'll end up finding your own way to the chuck wagon."

The spoon came to a halt within inches of her nose, and Delle leaned forward and sniffed, eyes closed in appreciation. "All this and sherry, too? Mmm, definitely a man for all seasons."

Cyrus's eyes crinkled. He laughed, and she joined in. "Go on before I change my mind," he said gruffly. "I don't take all my...all the renters under my wing, you know. Only the needier cases."

"I need, I need!" Delle exclaimed, still laughing as she moved into the living room area to clear aside newspapers and books. She made herself a nest among the pillows on the couch and settled herself, cross-legged, just as Cyrus brought two thick pottery bowls of the seafood bisque.

"Who made this stuff?" she asked several minutes later. "It's heavenly!"

"What do you mean, who made it?" Cyrus reached for the last slice of oven-made toast and tore it in half, offering her the largest piece. "Who do you think made it?"

"If you can cook like this, you're wasted down here. Did you ever think of going into the restaurant business? This place could use a good restaurant, and if the rest of your talents measure up to this sample..."

Tipping back his chair, Cyrus stretched his legs under the coffee table and surveyed her from under a sweep of thick, stubby lashes. His reply was long in coming, short when it came. "No thanks."

"Don't you have any ambition at all?"

"To do what?"

"To...well, to better yourself. To make something of your life." That had sounded like a criticism, and it hadn't been meant that way—at least, she didn't think it had. "What I meant was—" Breaking off, she sighed heavily.

Steepling his fingertips, Cyrus continued to study her. "Go on, don't be shy. I'd be interested in knowing your opinion of my life-style."

Backpaddling as gracefully as she could, Delle said, "Well, I don't really know much about it, do I? You do a little bit of this, a little bit of that. As you said, it's traditional, but still . . ."

"You know more about my life-style than I do about yours."

Was he asking? Delle didn't want to talk about herself. What she wanted was to prod this infuriatingly complacent man into *doing* something.

Neither of them spoke. The stillness held a quality of waiting. In a noisy flurry of sparks a log settled, and she twisted her bowl on the table, studying the incised design. "Compared to yours, my life's deadly dull."

"You don't have to offer beads and trinkets to the natives, you know," Cyrus said quietly. "Cash will do just fine."

She deserved that. All the same, it hurt. Why was it that every time they talked about anything more personal than hot water heaters or fishing rods, she came off sounding like a patronizing prig? An apology would probably only make things worse.

Cyrus's eyes were suddenly opaque, the color of the laurel bay that grew everywhere on the island. The dancing motes of light that she'd come to look for were nowhere in evidence, and she resigned herself to having seen the last of them. And of him.

"What made you go into banking?" he asked unexpectedly, and Delle, inordinately relieved, stopped fingering her bowl and began working on the wool fringe of the afghan.

"My oldest brother, actually," she confessed.

"The salmon fisherman?"

"They were all salmon fishermen," she said dryly. "And shooters of grouse. And pheasant. And anything else that could be smoked, frozen, stuffed or mounted."

"Is that why you were so dead set on catching a drum?"

"Certainly not! At least . . ." Lifting her eyes to his, she sighed. "Why is it that men insist on collecting trophies? Is it some masculine rite of passage? My father's den used to give me nightmares as a child. I dreaded going in there, but it was his favorite room of all. One of the senior vice presidents of our bank has a blue marlin mounted in his office that's longer than his desk, and I happen to know he gets deathly seasick if the water cooler gurgles when he passes by."

"Maybe his wife caught it. What do you collect?"

"Do I have to collect anything?"

"You strike me as the sort of woman who would."

"I'm not sure I like the sound of that. Are we talking matchbook covers or ritual shrunken heads?"

With every evidence of relaxing, Cyrus spread an arm along the back of the cushions. His eyes crinkled into the beginnings of a smile, and Delle found herself telling him about the doll collection she'd had as a child.

"Shelves and shelves of them. Games, too," she said. "Every time Father went on a trip, he'd bring me something. If he took the boys, I got a big, expensive doll. For a business trip, a game would do."

"You liked games?"

"Not really. There was no one to play them with. The dolls were better, especially the baby dolls. Costume dolls weren't good for much besides putting on a shelf and admiring, and after a while I forgot to admire them, but the others—every night before bedtime, I tucked in each doll, making sure its little limbs were straight and it was as comfortable as I could make it. Oren used to tease me unmercifully about that."

"Oren?"

"My brother. I have three, all older. Oren is thirty-five now, and he went into banking right out of school. Three years later he was elected a vice president."

Cyrus's thick, dark brows lifted. "Your role model?"

With a gesture of impatience, Delle uncrossed her legs and lowered them to the floor. She propped her arms across her knees, hunching her shoulders as she leaned over to stare at the braided rug. "Of course not. It's just that I happened to have been born into an all male household—"

"A minor miracle in itself, I'd say."

"What I meant was, my mother died when I was a child. Even before that, she was hardly a factor. I don't ever remember her voicing an opinion on anything except how I should wear my hair. She thought long curls and an Alice band would look pretty, but I ended up wearing braids."

Capturing his gaze as it skimmed thoughtfully over her hair, she grimaced. "Father's idea. God, I hated it! I looked like a baby rabbit—all ears and eyes."

"You had them fixed?"

"The ears? No, I grew into them." She could smile now in remembrance of the teasing she'd suffered at the hands of her brothers, all of whom had inherited their mother's small, flat ears. It hadn't been funny at the time. "I was supposed to have been another boy," she confided. "Actually, I wasn't supposed to be at all. A major slipup, you might say. After Mother died, I was bundled off to boarding school, where I spent some of the happiest years of my life." She paused, a look of surprise on her face. "How much sherry did you put in that soup, anyway? I *never* talk about personal matters."

"Just a few drops. So then you met your friends, the gulls," Cyrus cued, and she was off again.

"June got married in her last year at college, and then Hetty and Paula. Then it was my turn. I got engaged to Oren's best friend. My father's hand-picked candidate," she added wryly.

Cyrus found himself completely captivated by the subtle play of expression on her face. As skilled as he was at reading people, Delle Richardson was a challenge to him. He'd lay odds that she didn't open up this readily as a rule, and it was suddenly extremely important to him that she continue to talk about herself. God knows, most women did little else.

His silence held a careful blend of disinterest and invitation. It was a technique that often worked in dealing with troubled teenage boys, and he was gambling on its effectiveness now.

"You see, women are like poker chips," Delle explained gravely. "They're of little intrinsic value, but they can be traded for the real thing. In this case, the real thing was a rising young lawyer with an impeccable pedigree who happened to have inherited a third of the voting stock in a small company my father had been wanting for years."

Richardson. Richardson from Richmond, Virginia . . . that would be Cordell Richardson. Good Lord, the poor girl had been spawned by one of the hungriest sharks in the southeast!

"So you decided not to be cashed in and went to work, instead. Good for you." At the bleak little smile that flickered and was gone, he changed course. "Wrong?"

"Oh, it was the right decision," she assured him. "Only I didn't handle it very well. I ended up alienating my family and scandalizing all Father's friends. It was awful."

"You didn't love him enough?" It was none of his business, but as long as she was in a confiding mood, he was determined to get it all out of her. Nor did he care to delve too deeply into his motives.

"What did I know about love? I told you, all my friends were getting married—it was the thing to do." She smiled, and Cyrus caught a glimpse of the girl she must have been in the tender slope of her cheek, the vulnerability of her full lower lip.

"You were of age," he reminded her.

"A woman is never of age until she's married, according to my father. Anyway, Peter had taken me to all the school dances for years. When he asked me to marry him, it seemed only natural."

"How did it end?"

"Badly. I'd been having doubts for a long time, but I thought it was because we hadn't . . . you know. Made love. Peter wanted an early night after the rehearsal dinner, so I went home with Father, but later on, I slipped out and drove to Peter's apartment. He'd given me my own key just that night, and I thought it would be a lovely surprise to—" She swallowed hard. "The surprise was mine," she said, her voice thin with remembrance. "Peter was already entertaining—a woman."

"Jesus," Cyrus breathed softly.

"I left. They didn't see me, and when I told Father what had happened, do you know what he said? Bridal jitters! Nerves!" Her laughter was as wounding as broken glass. "Oren was there, and he was just as bad as Father. I told them I couldn't—that I didn't love Peter, and he obviously didn't care much for me. Cyrus, can a man do that? Love one woman enough to marry her and still want to sleep with another one?"

Slowly, he shook his head. "Delle, I can't speak for all men." The man who'd do that to her was crazy. The man who could even want another woman when he could have Delle . . .

"The wedding was the next day. . . . Oren kept going on about maintaining family ties, and obligations to old girlfriends, and Father was convinced that I was having an attack of nerves." She lifted her head, and Cyrus thought he'd never seen anything so heartbreakingly lovely as the long line of her throat, even with a mosquito bite or two.

"So you waited until it was almost too late," he stated.

"You can't know what it's like, growing up in a house where men are in the majority and men are always right. My stepmother wasn't allowed to voice an opinion, even if she'd had one." She uttered a broken laugh. "Of course, weighing a little thing like a prospective stepson-in-law's alleged infidelity against all she had to lose, I seriously doubt that she'd have spoken even if anyone had given her the chance."

"What about afterward?" Cyrus prompted. "I mean after you left him at the altar?"

"Technically, he left me. I told him I wasn't going to marry him as soon as I got to the altar, and suggested he and Oren slip out the side door. I don't know if he believed me or not—maybe it was guilty conscience, or maybe he was just afraid I'd embarrass him by throwing up in my bouquet. I was feeling pretty rocky. At any rate, he started edging away, and I told the guests that they were still invited to the reception, but that there wouldn't be a wedding. Most of them were Father's business friends, anyway, and the reception was supposed to pay back a lot of social obligations."

My God, he could just picture it! Talk about carrying it off in style.

"The gulls took care of me, no questions asked. Paula told Jeanette, my stepmother, to give back as many gifts as she could at the reception, and that they'd come back the next day and help take care of the rest. Then Hetty booked me into the hotel where they were staying, and June packed my clothes. The rest, as they say..."

"Is history? Friends like that are hard to come by. No wonder you're disappointed at not seeing them."

Actually, Delle discovered that she wasn't quite as disappointed as she might have been. Cyrus had managed to insinuate himself into her life more quickly than anyone had in years. Delle didn't make friends easily, but those she made, she kept.

Cyrus, watching her, decided it was time to end the session. He'd learned far more about her than he'd dared hope, but not nearly enough. Not yet. "Offhand, I'd say you've done pretty well for yourself. Good friends, a satisfying career, what more could a woman ask?"

Delle shot him a quick look. How many times had she asked herself the same question? She had yet to come up with an answer, but she was getting closer. She felt it in her bones. "A vacation," she suggested.

"It's yours. For as long as you want."

Delle rather doubted that, but it was sweet of him to offer. A day or so more, perhaps, and then New York. She was ready for it. In the two days she'd been here, she'd practically kicked the antacid habit; she was sleeping like a log, waking up refreshed instead of having to drag herself out of bed.

Collecting both soup bowls, Cyrus headed for the kitchen, congratulating himself for having pulled her out of her shell. All too soon the walls would go up again, he suspected. Next time she wouldn't be caught off guard so easily.

He halted in his tracks. Why did it matter so much? Hell, she wasn't one of his boys. And he was no psychiatrist, in spite of his success with some of the young toughs who'd learned a measure of self-respect under his guidance. All right, so she interested him—maybe a little too much. He could handle it. "I'm brewing us a special tea," he called over his shoulder.

"Cyrus, thanks, but I'm not a tea drinker."

"This is special," he repeated as he returned with the last of the soup. "Grows on the island, I cured it myself. Good for what ails you."

"Nothing ails me," Delle stressed. She leaned forward, her face once more closed. "Now, when do we go back after that fish?"

"Are you serious? I thought you'd had enough surf fishing to last you for a while."

"He got away. I'm not leaving here until I get my drum fish."

"Promise? Okay, we'll go out again tomorrow. I'll show you how to fish with bare hooks. The big ones are suckers for a bare hook."

Delia shot him a suspicious look. "Why do I get the feeling you're putting me on?"

"Me? Putting on a lady banker? A wheel of commerce?"

"All right, have your fun. Just because I'm successful at what I do, just because I've set certain goals for myself, you think I'm a joke, right?"

"Oh, heavens no," he declared gravely. "I think all that ambition is highly commendable."

Delle frowned. He was teasing her. She was certain of it ... almost. "It isn't every woman who's a vice president before she's thirty. I didn't even start out to be a banker, so I had to come from behind, you might say. Night classes and all that."

"Admirable."

"Cyrus, dammit—"

"You're up to ... what, a pack a day?"

"Cigarettes? I don't even smoke."

"Antacids."

"What are you, some kind of health nut?"

"You might say that."

"Well, take a bow. Thanks to you, I'm no longer in danger of starving. I might even consider eating breakfast on a regular basis."

Cyrus handed her a cup of green tea, and she peered at it suspiciously. "This is supposed to be good for me?"

"What do you usually drink after dinner?"

"Not green tea with little black things floating around in it, I can assure you." She sniffed it warily. "You know, this is getting to be an embarrassing habit, your rescuing me, drying me off and then feeding me."

"You hear anyone complaining?"

She sipped the tea and found it pleasant enough. He'd added a few drops of milk and sweetened it lightly, which helped. "As for all that other—the stuff I told you, forget it, will you? I haven't the faintest idea why I opened up like that. I *never* discuss personal matters."

Cyrus made no reply. Gradually, the stillness of the room grew into an awareness that prickled her nerve endings, and Delle stole a look at him.

He was staring directly at her, and she swallowed hard. "Yeah, I feel it, too," Cyrus said huskily, his smile slow in coming, almost as if he didn't want to smile at her.

"Feel it?" What she felt at that moment didn't bear analysis. He couldn't possibly be feeling what she was feeling. "Tea always makes me too warm." She placed her cup on the coffee table.

Cyrus rose and came around to where she sat. He held out a hand, and as if in a trance, she took it. Free will was a thing of the past. She found herself in far more danger of drowning in the green depths of his eyes than she had ever been in the surging tides of the Atlantic.

"It isn't the tea that's raising my temperature," he told her. "From the very first time I saw you, I've wanted to do this."

"To do what?" She knew...oh, God, yes, she knew! Yet she had to ask. Words were a device to delay the inevitable, to draw out this shimmering tension until it fused them into one molten lump.

"To kiss you. To taste your mouth, to hold you and feel the strength under all that fragile softness."

He was coming closer, and her eyelids drooped lazily. Breathlessly, she protested. "But that's crazy. It was only yesterday."

"Yesterday?" His arms slipped around her, but instead of crushing her to him, he held her gently, his gaze caressing her lips, her cheeks, the soft wings of her eyebrows.

Delle felt her fingers curl into the hard muscles of his chest, and she flattened her palms. It just made things worse—of their own volition, her hands slipped around his sides, under his arms.

She waited, hardly able to support her own weight as a sweet weakness invaded her lower limbs.

Cyrus sighed. "Yesterday, huh? Funny, I thought it had been longer than that. We'd better wait until tomorrow, at least." His voice sounded slightly strangled, as if he were having trouble controlling the flow of air, and Delle's eyes snapped open.

Was it her imagination, or was there a flush on those weathered cheeks of his? "Cyrus?" she whispered.

"I wouldn't want you to think I was rushing you."

Not until her lungs began to hurt did it occur to Delle that she'd forgotten to breathe. Dragging in a deep gulp of air, she regained enough composure to snatch her hands from his sides. She backed away, struggling against disappointment as she re-erected her toppled barriers. It was the sherry. It had to be the sherry—she'd only just met the man! "What time is the first ferry tomorrow?"

"What?"

"The ferry!" she repeated irritably.

"You're running away? Somehow, I'd have thought you had more courage than that," Cyrus said softly.

"It has nothing to do with courage," she muttered. "I'd planned to go on to New York for a few days, and if I leave now, I'll have that much longer to spend there. My secretary will have my appointments all lined up by now."

"That's your idea of a vacation?" Cyrus moved behind the bar that separated the living area from the kitchen and began doing something with the dishes. Delle took advantage of the opportunity to regain control over her emotions. She was not an emotional woman. Lapses of this sort made her uncomfortable.

"It's not vacation, it's business." She turned away to stare out the window. The palm tree—that poor, ludicrous palm tree. Whose idea had that thing been? It was no more indigenous to these parts than—than *she* was.

At least the sexual tension had fled, if it had ever been there. She'd probably imagined the whole thing. Her imagination had been playing some pretty weird tricks on her lately—and yet, Cyrus had reacted to it, too.

"Business, hmm?" he murmured from the kitchen. "The woman with the cast-iron schedule. Pity you can't order cast-iron body components to replace those you're so determined to wear out."

As her temper flared, Delle felt the familiar burning sensation in her stomach. She blamed it on the noxious brew he'd made her drink. "Who do you think you are, God's gift to the working woman? You come here to patch a leaky roof and end up prescribing boiled weeds and a whole new life-style?"

"It's the least I can do," he said with irritatingly false modesty.

"Oh yeah? Well, if you're so smart, why aren't you—"

"Rich?"

"If the shoe fits." She shrugged, tossing one bad cliché after another. It was hardly Cyrus's fault he'd been born into a life where opportunities were scarce. How would any one of her brothers have fared if fate had switched their circumstances? Still, other men had left these islands and made something of their lives. On Hatteras or Ocracoke he might have had more of a chance, but on Coranoke? The only business here was Lavada's store, and the island hardly supported even that.

"I guess the shoe fits, but then I never cared much for shoes." Cyrus dried the stock pot and reached for the denim jacket he'd worn over his jeans and sweatshirt. "As for riches, I have all I need, lady banker."

Delle stared across the pine counter at him, seeing the high forehead under a crop of thick, sun-bleached hair, the keen eyes and sensitive mouth. Whatever else he was, Cyrus Burrus was a proud man, and she'd attacked that pride time after time by her thoughtless remarks.

The crazy thing was, Delle *never* made thoughtless remarks. She'd learned long ago to be extremely deliberate in all she did or said. Something about this man simply destroyed her better judgment. It was as if his very independence were a threat to her own security.

Long after Cyrus had disappeared into the woods behind her cottage, Delle's thoughts lingered on him. She'd seen physically attractive men before, well-dressed men who drove expensive cars and frequented the best clubs and restaurants. She'd never been more than mildly interested—certainly not interested enough to risk getting involved.

With Cyrus... She shook her head, mystified. What *was* it with Cyrus, anyway? It wasn't what he wore. It certainly wasn't what he drove. Yet the more she was with him, the more impressed she was with his quiet, inner strength. There was a stability about him that drew her like a magnet. It was more than just his looks, although Lord knows, those were trouble enough.

Delle concluded finally that it was his strength. Her father was a strong man, too, but whereas his strength took the form of cold, relentless ambition, Cyrus's strength took the form of gentleness. Of the two, Cyrus's was by far the more dangerous to a woman determined to remain uninvolved.

Restlessly, she prowled the small cottage. When the walls began to close in on her, she let herself out into the screened porch. It would be shady in the summertime, sheltered in the winter. The muffled roar of the sea was pervasive, more a throbbing in her bones than a sound in her ears. She lowered herself into the hammock that stretched across one corner, wishing belatedly that she'd brought along a blanket. She could grow addicted to this sort of comfort.

Who was the painter who'd succumbed to island fever? Gauguin? There were probably dozens of others, she mused—hundreds, in fact. There was something about being on an island that stripped away pretenses. It could easily undermine purpose, too, she suspected.

Later—she never knew exactly how much later—Delle opened her eyes, cold and disoriented. The phone was ringing inside the cottage, and cautiously, she lowered her feet to the floor and sat up.

This salt air was really getting to her! All she seemed able to do was sleep and eat.

"I'm coming, I'm coming," she grumbled, hurrying inside to snatch up the phone.

"I thought if I let it ring long enough you'd hear it. Haven't you girls run down yet?"

"Oren?" She recognized her brother's voice immediately. "Is Father all right?" Her father was a prime candidate for a stroke, but nothing anyone could say would make him slow down.

"Working on his chip shot last time I saw him. He and Jeanette are leaving for Palm Springs next week."

"Terrific. Did Jeanette lock his office and throw away the key? How did you track me down, anyway?" If there was an edge of resentment in her voice, Delle didn't bother to hide it. She'd had little time to spare for her family over the past few years, but then, they'd had little for her, either.

"I got your number from the bank."

"Daniel had orders not to—"

"Cordelia, do you think I don't know how to get a phone number from a secretary?" Oren said witheringly. "Anyhow, I'd planned to stop by and see you on my way down here yesterday. You can imagine my surprise—"

"Down where?"

"I'm at Hatteras with a few friends. We've chartered a boat for the weekend."

Delle made a silent vow to get back to the beach at the first possible opportunity. Whatever Oren managed to catch from a boat, she could darn well catch more of and bigger from the shore!

"What are you doing down on Coranoke? Interviewing for corporate trust manager of the Coranoke National Bank? I hear the population over there is thirty-seven people, thirty-three billion ticks and twice that many mosquitoes."

"Very funny. How's Connie?" She'd always wondered why such a nice woman had married such a horrible man.

"As always, busy with good works. Look, Sis, we'll be going out to the Gulf Stream in the morning, but we should be back in by about four or five. Why not come on over and have dinner? It's been more than six months since I've seen you."

"We've both been busy. Are Worth and Jonathan all right?" Hearing her oldest brother's voice brought about a small surge of guilt. Both Oren and her father had sided with Peter six years before, but family was family, and they were all she had.

"Worth's getting balder and Jonathan's having marital problems. We'll catch up on the news over dinner."

"Dinner's a problem. The last ferry leaves Hatteras for Coranoke at five-thirty."

"No problem at all. If I can't get you a ride back across the inlet, I'll book you a room at our motel. Come on, Sis, you can snap pictures of our catch—did you bring along a wide-angle lens?''

"How about a magnifying lens?" Delle scoffed. She'd brought along her camera, but it was probably stiff from disuse. Still, Oren might be able to give her a few pointers before she went to New York to look over the two banks she was considering. The rosy pictures painted by the headhunters were one thing; a view from a disinterested third party might be more useful.

Oren gave her the name of the boat they'd chartered and told her how to find the marina. Delle promised to be waiting to photograph his catch. She had no intention of spending the night there, but surely she could hire someone to run her back to Coranoke.

She hung up, a little surprised at the resentment she felt at the intrusion.

Intrusion? Her vacation was almost over, at least as far as Coranoke was concerned. If she were smart, she'd load up her car, catch the midday ferry, dine with Oren and then drive on back to Norfolk. She could be in her own bed shortly after midnight, with time to check by the bank before taking off for New York. If she wasn't satisfied with what she found in New York, there'd still be time to check out Atlanta.

Cyrus stapled another batt of insulation overhead and paused to flex his aching back muscles. Time to call it a night. There'd be plenty of time to finish the new dormitory before summer, but he'd learned long ago never to put things off. Work had a way of piling up, and first thing you knew, the pressure was back. Pressure was something he could do without.

Climbing down the ladder, he dropped the heavy-duty stapler in the tool box and dusted off his hands. The trouble with this kind of work was that it left a man too free to think. And thoughts sometimes led down nonproductive pathways.

What was Delle doing at this moment, he wondered. Packing to leave?

He was beginning to wish she'd never come in the first place. She was the last thing he needed to meet at this point in his life. Far too intriguing to ignore, but too driven with ambition to risk getting involved with.

Ambition could be a hell of a jockey once it got its spurs in a man's flanks. Or a woman's, he acknowledged with a wry smile. It had almost ridden him into the ground before he'd thrown it off. Unless he missed his guess, Delle was headed down the same track.

When he'd sold out and left Charlotte, his friends had all thought he'd lost his mind. Instead, he'd found it. He'd lost a hell of a lot, but he'd found something far more valuable. He'd discovered that happiness was a matter of attitude and values rather than position and possessions. Money wouldn't buy it. At least, not for him. Not for Delle Richardson, either, unless he missed his guess. Only that wasn't something you could tell a person. The knowledge had to come from inside.

Cyrus glanced around at the barren room that would one day house six boys. One of the wags at the social services office he dealt with had called it another halfway house—halfway between jail and summer camp. He got the hard cases, the kids who fell through the cracks in the system. Too young for jail, but too tough for foster homes. Six weeks was all the time he had to instill a spark of self-respect, self-confidence and self-reliance in them, and he didn't kid himself that he accomplished it in every case. At least he tried. From here they went on to other places of a similar nature, where they could stay for as long as a year or more.

Revenge had been all he could think of when he'd confronted the young punks who'd trashed his apartment, spray painted half his art collection, defaced his books and smashed a collection of museum-quality glasswork. He'd felt utterly violated.

Revenge had been out of the question, considering their ages and circumstances. After three weeks of scourging his soul, he'd known what he had to do. It had taken almost a year to change the course of his life, but he'd never once regretted it.

Just for a moment when Delle had been talking about her relationship with her family and what had almost happened as a result, he'd been reminded of that senseless act of destruction. How could anyone in their right mind take something so lovely, so intrinsically fine, and willfully destroy it?

Soaping himself down under the shower, Cyrus's thoughts veered off in another direction.

Women. There were a few he'd seen on an irregular basis, one on Ocracoke, a couple on Hatteras. Summer women. Regulars who rented for a week or a month each year. He could as easily have dated a winter woman, but he'd never met one he cared enough for. The summer ones weren't looking for permanence.

The winters were short, but they were fierce and bleak. A man got hungry for the sound and feel and smell of a woman.

Fortunately, he had enough to keep him busy. It helped. Fiberglassing his boat, keeping abreast of the repairs on the rental cottages that supported his summer camp, gill netting, occasionally doing some long hauling when he had someone to fish with him.

A couple of times a year he tried to scrape off enough barnacles to spend a few days in town, if only to remind himself of what it was he'd given up. Three days of city traffic, with all the attendant hassles, and he was usually ready to head for the island again.

And then along came Delle Richardson, at a time when he was almost caught up with his work and the drum run was just beginning to come in. Suddenly, he forgot all about fishing, all about delinquent kids and all about hassles with the IRS, who couldn't accept the fact that a man had gone from a six-figure income to something just slightly above the poverty level in a single year.

All he could think of was the way she'd looked in that chocolate colored satin thing she'd been wearing when he climbed down off her roof. Regal as a duchess, mad as a hornet...altogether the most stunning woman he'd ever laid eyes on.

Cyrus had sense enough to know that it was probably largely physical, but knowing it didn't help. Most relationships began as a physical attraction. What if there were more? What if he got hooked on her? If there was one thing he couldn't afford at this point in his life, it was involvement with a woman like Delle. She didn't fit into his world, and he was damned sure he could no longer fit into hers.

Six

___

Delle worked the shutter of her camera until she was satisfied with its action. She loaded it, checked to see that her spare lenses were still in their cases and carried the bag out to her car. All morning she'd been toying with the notion of simply packing everything and leaving Coranoke for good. It was time. God knows, it would be simpler.

Safer, too, whispered an inner voice. Six years ago she'd deliberately stepped into a world of neat little figures, neat little facts, a world where everything added up, leaving no untidy loose ends.

Cyrus Burrus didn't add up. He frightened her. No, to be quite honest, he fascinated her. It was the fascination that frightened her.

In case he decided to make another unannounced visit, Delle left the cottage early, strolling in the opposite direction from the one she'd already explored. Now and then she paused to lift her camera, hoping she wouldn't be caught in the act. Delle and her Nikon had once been a familiar sight on two campuses. She'd started out in the eighth grade as a yearbook photographer, and ended up as picture editor for her college annual. She'd had a knack for capturing both the nostalgic and the outrageous.

But it was different here among these somber live oaks, where a man's yard not only enclosed his castle, but his collard patch, his boats and even the graves of his ancestors. She felt like an intruder, and yet she found it impossible to resist the challenge.

Once, a lifetime ago, Delle had planned to become a photojournalist. That dream had long since gone the way of all dreams, but there was no reason why she couldn't get back into photography, if only as a means of relaxing some of the tension produced by the discipline of her work.

Shortly before noon she returned to the cottage, making a pot of coffee and a bread and butter sandwich. Then she changed into one of her two remaining dry outfits, a raw silk safari-style suit with a splashy red and gold print shirt underneath, all the while subconsciously listening for Cyrus. She'd seen nothing of him all day.

The drive to the landing took only a couple of minutes. Delle cast a wistful glance over her shoulder and then drove her car on board. Once again she was the only passenger on the free state-run ferry. After they pulled away from the island, she got out of her car and leaned over the rail to watch the hundreds of pelicans drifting on the glassy surface of the water. For their part, they largely ignored her. She reset her lens for the incredible brightness and snapped a dozen shots. At least she'd have a memento of this vacation.

With time to spare, she explored the lower three villages on Hatteras Island, shooting two rolls of film and loading her last one while she waited at the marina for Oren's boat to maneuver into position at the dock.

There were pennants flying from the outriggers of several of the boats, proclaiming their catch, but none from his. Delle smiled as she strolled over to meet him.

Oren was the first one off the boat. She didn't recognize the man who disembarked next, which didn't surprise her. Oren never did anything for sheer pleasure. He'd be a client, making the whole trip a write-off.

It was the third man who captured her attention, and Delle's eyes widened in disbelief. She'd already covered half the distance between the marina office and the dock, but now she stopped in her tracks.

Peter? God, it was! How could he have—

"Oren," she said, seething as her brother sauntered over to where she stood rooted, "that's Peter!"

"Sure it is, Delle, didn't I tell you? I thought I'd mentioned it." Even with his lips and nose thickly plastered with a protective coating of ointment, Oren's long-featured face had a patrician look.

"You know damned well you didn't mention it! How *could* you have done this to me?"

"Delle, no one's done anything to you," her brother said tiredly. "I set up the trip for the CEO of Orico-Atlantic, and Peter happens to be a mutual friend. It seemed logical to invite him along."

"You mean the two of you are joining forces to put over one of your deals," she accused. "Does the poor man know how you two trade off clients?"

"You're overreacting, Delle. You always did, you always will. Just because you chose not to marry Peter—"

"You mean just because *he* chose to go directly from our rehearsal supper to that—that slut!"

Oren's long, slender fingers bit into her arm as he led her away from where the others were off-loading several ice chests. "Actually, she was a nice woman, and she and Peter had been seeing each other for years. She wasn't the sort a man would marry, but that doesn't mean—"

"My God, you sound like something out of a Regency novel."

"Delle, you're acting like an hysterical child. I'd hoped that after all these years, you'd grown up, but I'm beginning to wonder if you ever will."

"If by growing up you mean that I'll learn to look the other way when someone displays a complete lack of moral scruples, I hope I never grow up."

"I keep telling you, it had nothing to do with morals. It had nothing to do with you and Peter."

"I'm not talking about me, I'm talking about that poor woman who—what was it you said? A nice woman, but not the sort a man would marry?"

All around them were the sounds and smells of a busy marina. Laughter, the clank of a bucket against concrete, cars passing by on nearby Highway 12. Delle drew in a deep breath, filling her lungs with air that smelled of fish and saltwater and diesel fuel.

"Poor Father. He was really heartbroken, wasn't he? All those lovely shares of Remington-Dunn. His fingers were itching to get them in the family...." She laughed bitterly, oblivious of the incongruity of their surroundings. "Oren, I'm your sister. I was twenty-two years old, and the man I was supposed to marry within a few hours was lying there jaybird naked in bed with another woman. How do you think I felt?"

Displacing his terry-cloth cap, Oren ran his fingers through his thinning hair. "You had no business barging into Peter's apartment that way. Look, Delle, this is neither the time nor the place for rehashing old injuries, real or imagined. Come on, drive me back to the motel so I can shower, and then we'll have a nice, civilized drink and talk about what's going on in your life over dinner. Grapevine has it that you've been thinking about moving north. Are you sure this is the time to make a move? It'll set you back at least—"

"I've lost my appetite."

"Delle. Shoptalk, all right? Nothing else, I promise."

Even in sunscreen and unlaced deck shoes, Oren was intimidating. Years of conditioning couldn't be undone all at once. But he was her brother, and they did have a profession in common. Delle led the way to her car, determined to show him that she was no longer a timid child he could alternately tease and ignore.

The motel was located right on the beach. Instead of waiting inside while Oren showered and changed, Delle chose to wait for him on the boardwalk that led over the top of the dunes. She'd already missed the last ferry; she was stuck here for the time being. Besides, she rationalized, if she couldn't hold her own with her brother, she was certainly no match for New York. In her most brutally honest moments, Delle knew that she'd more or less patterned herself after Oren. He was the most ruthless of her brothers, much more like their father than the others. Which was probably the reason he was the favorite, she thought wryly.

Leaving her tan flats on the top of the dune, she wandered down to the surf. The wind was much cooler here than at Coranoke, the whole island more exposed.

Exposed and vulnerable. Just as she'd been all those years ago when she'd almost let herself be pushed into marriage with her brother's closest friend.

Peter's family was even wealthier than her own. Somewhere midway through her senior year at college, he'd suddenly ceased being familiar old Peter and turned into a fairytale prince. Self-induced illusions. She'd been ready for romance, and Peter had been there, the same friendly, obliging fellow who'd escorted her to all the dances at her father's request. Father, of course, had been worried about her getting mixed up with an "unsuitable type."

Delle hadn't known about her father's efforts to buy his way into R-D & Co., a small but highly successful manufacturer of aircraft interiors. But she'd found out. Just as she'd found out how little her own happiness meant to the male members of her family.

Fighting nausea, she'd raced back home that night and charged into her father's study. "Father, I am not getting married tomorrow."

Even in his shirt sleeves, with cigar ashes on his vest, Cordell Richardson was an imposing figure. Jeanette had appeared in the doorway, and he'd waved her away. "What foolishness is this, last-minute nerves? Cordelia, you've known Peter all your life. He comes from good stock, and you're fortunate to have a man of his caliber to look after your interests."

"My interests! Is that what he was doing tonight?" Still in shock, she'd blurted out what she'd just seen. "Father, how could he do it if he loves me? We've never slept together—Peter's never even *asked* me to go to bed with him!"

"My dear Cordelia, there are two kinds of women," her father had informed her, and she'd told him what he could do with his "two kinds of women."

"There are a thousand-zillion kinds of women," she'd stormed. "What difference does *that* make?"

Oren had joined them then, and together they'd almost managed to make her believe she'd misunderstood what she'd seen. She'd slept until nearly noon the next day, when Hetty, Paula and June had come to help her dress. Her friends had stayed at a hotel because the Richardson guest rooms were filled by Oren's fiancée down from Connecticut for the wedding, two elderly cousins, and Jonathan and Worth and their wives.

Seeming as lifeless as one of the dolls that lined the shelves in her room, Delle had allowed herself to be hooked and buttoned and snapped into smothering layers of silk. A dozen times she'd opened her mouth to say she couldn't go through with it, and each time she'd closed it again, fighting the nausea that came over her in waves.

Nerves, her father had called it. Perhaps it was. Perhaps she'd dreamed the whole thing. An hour later, she'd walked slowly down the aisle on her father's arm—step, pause, step, pause—head held high. She'd desperately wanted to believe it was all a bad dream, but it was no use. The closer she'd come to the flower-banked altar where Peter waited, the sicker she'd felt. By the time her father released her arm and stepped away, she'd known what she had to do.

"Dear God," she whispered now to the seething surf, "I can't believe I was ever such a spineless ninny."

Dining with Oren was no real treat at the best of times, and tonight would probably be no different, Delle told herself. Still, he was her brother. There'd been a couple of years when she'd thought no one in her family would ever speak to her again, and at the time, that had suited her just fine.

Actually, the evening began well enough. They talked shop, and Delle welcomed Oren's advice about the importance of attitude when moving into a new situation. She was still at the same bank where she'd started as a junior account officer, her experience lamentably lacking in some areas.

They were already into their shrimp cocktails when Peter and his companion were shown to a table not ten feet away. Delle glanced up at her brother to see him watching her warily.

"Is this your idea of entertainment, Oren? What were you expecting, tears? Tantrums?" Her cocktail fork clattered against her service plate.

"Delle, I swear to you, I didn't know they were coming here. I thought they'd eat at the Quarterdeck, where we ate last night. Anyway, what difference does it make? Don't you think you're overreacting?"

"Overreacting!" Couldn't he understand anything? It wasn't seeing Peter again after all these years that upset her—it was the thought that her own brother could be so unfeeling.

"Delle, it's been six years. The family managed to survive the scandal, and I daresay Richmond's forgotten about it by now. Peter's been married, divorced, and he's married again, and you've had nothing but good luck in your career."

"Good *luck*? Oren, have you always been so obtuse, or have you just been out in the sun too long?"

"Just teasing, little sister. You've come a long way, and I'm proud of you. We all are."

Delle relented. Perhaps she had overreacted, but she refused to let him off the hook so easily. "Before you get too stuffy and condescending, big brother, let me remind you that I made VP in three-and-a-half months less time than you did, and I didn't start with an MBA from Wheaton."

"Ah, but you had all those lovely equal employment opportunity laws on your side."

Delle speared her last shrimp and bit through it. "Laws, my foot. I'm a quick study and a hard worker. Business math almost killed me, but I got my MBA the hard way—at night, holding down a full-time job. And with no help from EEOC, either."

"Chip off the old block, aren't you?"

She shot him a scathing look. "Am I supposed to be flattered?"

"You could do worse."

"That's your opinion. What arrangements have you made for getting me back to Coranoke?" she asked as she tackled the broiled bluefish the waitress had just placed before her. "Your charter boat?"

"Sorry—the skipper's gone to Manteo on personal business, but why not stay over? Our motel has plenty of vacancies. In fact, why not go out to the Stream with us tomorrow?"

"No thanks. You fish your way, I'll fish mine."

"And I'll catch a big one before you," Oren sang to the tune of *Loch Lomond*. "You've turned into quite a fighter, baby sister. You used to be such a docile little girl, all pigtails and big ears, playing with your dolls."

"Docile little girls have a way of getting trampled underfoot by the big boys if they don't learn to stay three steps ahead of them."

They talked shop during the rest of the meal, both of them careful not to jeopardize the fragile armistice between them. It was only later, while Oren was waiting for change at the front of the restaurant, that Delle decided to wipe the slate clean once and for all.

She strolled back to the table where Peter was just beginning his dinner. She'd felt his eyes on her several times during the evening, and had deliberately ignored him. His back was toward her now, and he was saying something to his gray-bearded companion.

"Hello, Peter, nice to see you again."

He swiveled around, his eyes widening. As she waited for him to swallow a big bite of fried fish, Delle began to smile. His scalp was sunburned. It gleamed like pink patent leather through his carefully combed dark hair.

Rocking back his chair, Peter Remington-Dunn got to his feet, and the other man followed suit. Delle acknowledged the introductions and then turned back to the man she'd almost married.

How odd—she felt absolutely nothing. No animosity, not even curiosity. "I just wanted to say hello, Peter. Please go on with your dinner before your fish gets cold."

"Delle! Won't you...uh..."

"I'd better be getting back to Coranoke if I want to be on the beach bright and early in the morning. I lost a really big drum yesterday, and I'm determined not to go home without him."

"Oh, you're into surf fishing now?"

"I'm into a lot of things now, Peter," she said gently. Six years ago her interests had been mainly parties, pretty clothes and good times. They'd both done a lot of changing. "It was nice seeing you again."

Oren appeared behind her, his eyes guarded, and she smiled impishly up at him. Poor sweet, what had he expected, the woman-scorned routine? "Ready to go?" She tucked her arm under his. "We'd better get back to the marina, Oren. Good luck tomorrow, Peter."

She'd just unlocked the door of her car when Peter emerged from the restaurant, blotting his mouth with a handkerchief as he hurried after her.

"Delle, wait up a minute, will you? I wanted to say...."

His words carried him halfway across the paved apron, and she turned and waited while Oren reluctantly let himself into the car. "Yes?" she prompted, when he seemed to be having trouble remembering what it was he wanted to say. In fact, he appeared to have a fish bone stuck in his throat.

In his place, Delle decided sympathetically, she'd be embarrassed, too. She knew for a fact that Oren had told him what had happened that night. What an embarrassing thing for a man to have on his conscience.

"Look, Delle, what I wanted to say was—well, I probably should have explained about—I mean, what I meant to say was..."

Delle lifted her hand to rest her fingertips lightly on his arm. She could afford to be generous. "Peter—don't," she said softly. "It's no longer important. We were two different people then, and we've both grown far beyond all that. I've forgotten all about it, and I hope you will, too."

Peter sighed heavily and covered her hand with his. "Of course, my dear, I just wanted to say that—well, it's all right. I understand, Delle, and I forgave you years ago."

She blinked. Spots swarmed past her eyes. Her fingers curled into fists, and she opened her mouth to annihilate the miserable worm who had the temerity to forgive *her* for *his* misdeeds. "Peter—" she managed finally.

And then she choked up. Spinning away, she slammed herself into her car, switched on the engine and backed recklessly out of the parking slot.

Beside her, Oren hastily fastened his shoulder harness, giving her a wary look. "Care to tell me what that was all about?" he asked just before they reached his motel.

"Didn't you hear? That's what you get for having such tiny ears." She breathed heavily, dark eyes glinting with indignation. "Your friend is a triple-A jerk. He was a jerk six years ago and he hasn't changed one bit!"

"There you go again, Delle," Oren said with a sigh. "Getting hysterical over nothing."

"Nothing! *Nothing?* Do you know what that nonentity had the nerve to say to me?" She wheeled into the parking lot, blocking three cars as she screeched to a halt near Oren's unit. "He forgives me. *He* forgives *me*!"

"Now, Delle, you really did put poor Pete in an embarrassing situation."

Delle searched for something devastating to say and then gave up. She didn't care anymore. Her father had said there were two kinds of women. Well, if that were true—not that she bought that chauvinistic old saw for one minute—then it was equally true that there were two kinds of men. And she knew damn well that Peter's kind wasn't worth a fraction of the emotional energy she'd expended on him. "Are you going to call the marina and find me a ride back to Coranoke, or shall I?"

"I'll call," Oren grumbled.

Ten minutes later, Delle snatched the phone book and scanned the page. "Dammit, you should have made arrangements before the place closed up for the night," she snapped, slamming the book shut and reaching for the phone.

Cyrus had said it would take him about forty-five minutes. Delle didn't care how long it took just so he was on his way. She'd left Oren at the motel and driven back to the marina, and it occurred to her now that she'd have to leave her car here and collect it later.

That didn't matter either. All that mattered was getting back to the cottage, back to Coranoke. Back to Cyrus. By the time she spotted the running lights of a boat in the distance, that simple need had become a full-blown compulsion.

Standing at the edge of the wharf, Delle did her best to put her feelings into perspective. Seeing Peter again had been a vindication of her earlier decision—not that she'd needed vindication. At least she knew now that there was nothing in her past to fear. There never had been, only she'd been too busy all these years to realize that simple fact.

This restlessness that had come over her these past few days had nothing to do with Peter or with any major career moves in the offing. The fact was that she'd allowed herself to become dangerously attracted to a man her father would have deemed completely unsuitable.

"We have absolutely nothing in common," she whispered as she watched the sleek white shape emerge from the darkness. "What am I going to do?"

The muffled sound of a wet exhaust took on a different note as the boat slipped between the two arms of the breakwater that protected Hatteras Harbor. Delle stood at the edge of the dock, waiting...wondering. What *was* it about the man? This thing she felt was more than just a physical reaction to his obvious masculine attractions. Surely she was too smart to be caught in that particular trap.

There was something solid about Cyrus Burrus, something steady and reassuring. Compared to him, all the men she'd ever known paled into insignificance. If that meant what she was afraid it did, then she was in serious trouble.

The ghostly white shape glided quietly alongside, the low throb of the engines loud against the sparkling silence. Delle resisted the urge to hurl herself into Cyrus's arms. Just barely. "Cyrus, I'm sorry, but I didn't know what else to do."

"Miscalculate the ferry schedule?" He reached up to help her down, and then moved back to the controls, reversing the engines.

"Miscalculated the alternatives," Delle corrected. "I came over to meet my brother after he assured me he'd arrange a ride back across the inlet after dinner."

"No problem. Glad to be of service."

Standing at the wheel, his feet braced apart, Cyrus left the harbor behind and headed west-southwest. Delle huddled in the stern, her eyes on the silhouette of his lean, muscular body against a white bulkhead, his head and shoulders against a star-studded sky.

Steady, reliable, strong. Those were the words she'd used to describe him in her mind, but she'd left out so much more. The laughter that danced in his sea-green eyes, the thick, sun-streaked hair that always looked windblown for the simple reason that it always was.

The gentleness that seemed so at odds with such rough-hewn strength.

"Cold?" he called softly over his shoulder. "It's warmer up here out of the wind."

Delle had no doubt that he was right. She could grow warm just thinking about it. With a sense of fatalism, she left the stern and moved the few feet across the cockpit to stand beside him in the shelter of the cuddy. Heat radiated from his body, a heat she could feel through the layers of clothing that separated his flesh from hers.

A trillion stars, give or take a few million, reflected like tiny diamonds on the dark, still water. They approached a channel marker, its red light reflecting endlessly, like a trail of rubies, to add to the illusion.

Delle shivered, and Cyrus wrapped an arm around her, drawing her close against his side. When she leaned her head on his shoulder, he said reassuringly, "It won't be much longer. We'll be home in a few minutes."

Home. A figure of speech. "It's beautiful," Delle murmured. "I could go on forever this way."

"Knowing you, you'd soon be hungry, and I didn't stock up. I know what you mean, though," he added quietly. "Suspended out here between two layers of stars, things take on a different perspective."

Or no perspective at all. Delle found herself suddenly incapable of putting together two consecutive rational thoughts. She was all awareness, her senses heightened to an incredible degree. The throb of the engines transmitted itself through the soles of her feet, setting off the craziest vibrations in the craziest places!

"Delle..." Cyrus's deep voice registered along her spine, adding to the effect. Moving abruptly, he made an adjustment to the controls, and then they were coasting on a sea of silence, coming to drift over infinitesimal swells just outside Coranoke's tiny harbor.

There was no wind to speak of, and here in the protection of the wooded island, little current. Cyrus turned to her then, their coming together as inevitable as the daybreak. "Oh, God, I've longed for this," he groaned just before his mouth covered hers.

He tasted of salt and sun, with a sweetness that was all his own. Delle was lost even before the kiss deepened into a wild and hungry joining. The muscles of his powerful arms bit into her flesh, but she managed to slip one arm around his waist, the other about his neck.

Both breathing heavily, they broke apart. Cyrus stared down at her wonderingly. Delle lifted a trembling hand to stroke his lean jaw, thrilling to the sandpapery texture, and Cyrus captured her finger between his teeth, stroking the sensitive pad with a hot, moist tongue until what little strength she still possessed threatened to melt away. The belt of her jacket had come unknotted under his deft fingers, and when she felt his hand slip under her blouse to stroke her bare back, Delle shuddered.

"I wish it were summertime," he whispered against that incredible erogenous curve where her neck joined her shoulder. "You wouldn't be wearing so many clothes."

"I'll be back next summer. No matter where I am by then," she whispered.

"Honey, I'm only human. Summer's a long time away."

Delle couldn't see, but she knew the lights were dancing in his eyes again. "I'm here now," she reminded him, and he groaned, crushing her against him until she felt the air rushing from her lungs.

"I know, I know!" His hand moved down to the waistband of her slacks and paused, unable to go farther. "Haven't you ever heard of elastic?"

Laughter came easily to join the wild flux of emotions that coursed through her. Delle dipped her fingers just under the unbelted waist of his jeans, savoring the sudden change from the hard, heated muscles of his back, to the cooler, more resilient flesh of his buttocks. He wore his pants low on his hips. "Haven't you?" she returned, her breath catching in delicious shock as she felt the immediate response of his body.

Cyrus captured her laughter in a kiss as his hands curved over her hips. He moved her against his hardened contours, making it all the worse for them both.

"Sweetheart, I can't last much longer," he said huskily. Control had never been a problem before—but then, he'd never known a woman like Delle. "Don't you know what you're doing to me?" His hands moved feverishly from her hips, up to her silken hair and back down again as he struggled to regain his balance.

"I—I think it's mutual," Delle gasped, burying her face in his damp throat.

"Is it? Are you sure?" he murmured unsteadily. God, listen to him! He couldn't even control his voice, much less his body. He was playing with dynamite and he couldn't seem to do a damned thing about it. Delle was no summer woman, in spite of what she'd intimated.

She wasn't a winter woman, either, so where did that leave them?

He slipped his hand around to the velvet softness of her stomach. He should have brought along a chaperon, dammit! He should have sent someone else to collect her. He should have...

His palm moved up over her stomach until it came to a scrap of lace, and he knew a surge of impatience with all the barriers that blocked access to his goal. All his hard-won common sense, the cool judgment that had once enabled him to reshape his whole life, disappeared. From a level that he'd never even known existed came a need so strong that he felt threatened by it. He wanted her—God, he wanted her so badly. They'd work things out between them later. Somehow.

His hand claimed a victory, and he felt her response. The tiny nugget probed his sensitive palm. "I'll take care of you, love," he crooned half under his breath, the words taking on new meaning even as they left his lips.

They were still standing in the shelter of the cuddy, leaning against the console. "Cyrus, this is crazy," Delle said helplessly.

"It's only crazy if you try to think about it, so don't think, Delle. We'll think things through tomorrow."

"You're being completely irresponsible, you know," she pointed out, her hands intent on a tour of discovery.

"Yeah, I know. Don't you wonder why?"

Delle was no longer interested in analyzing the situation. If she waited for a return of common sense, she might never know what was at the end of the rainbow. In thrall to a sweet compulsion that was more powerful than anything she'd ever known, she whispered against his lips, "Right you are, Rhett, we'll think about it tomorrow."

Moving silently, Cyrus released an anchor into the dark, silent waters. "I don't want to wake up in someone's pound net in the morning."

"I guess you might call this a shipboard romance," Delle ventured. Without Cyrus's arms about her, she was beginning to feel uncertain again.

"Think so?" he replied enigmatically. He was doing something with the lights, and Delle stood awkwardly by, telling herself that if she wanted to back out, this was her chance.

Her chance was short-lived. Cyrus swept an arm around her and led her below, and at his touch, she began to melt all over again.

"Incense?"

"Juniper. Sweetest wood there is, and the best for boat building. The bunk's over here."

"Cyrus, I—"

"Second thoughts?" he suggested gently. He'd deliberately forced himself to back off and give her time. Scruples could be a hell of a handicap, but with every moment that passed, he was more certain that this was no casual thing. If he took her now, neither of them would be able to walk away and forget it. She was right—it was crazy. But it was happening, all the same.

When she didn't reply, he pressed her down onto the padded bunk and sat beside her, leaving space between them. "Delle, do you trust me?"

"Of course I trust you," she snapped. Strangely enough, she did.

"Then you know I'd never do anything to hurt you. If you've changed your mind, I'll understand."

Delle shook her head, hopelessly confused. Why was he giving her a choice? Dammit, why hadn't he simply swept her off her feet? "Look, it's probably not a very good idea, Cyrus. I, uh—don't really go in for this sort of thing."

"I never thought you did," he said with quiet dignity. "Not that it would matter. But it's different with us, Delle, and I think you know it. It might not happen tonight, but sooner or later—"

She twisted abruptly away. "Sooner or later! Cyrus, you seem to forget that I'll be leaving here tomorrow." She felt like crying, for no other reason than sheer, frustrating disappointment. How dare he bring her this far and then give her the option of saying no!

"It just won't work," she said, sighing heavily.

"It could. If we wanted it badly enough." Cyrus found her hand and began toying with her fingers.

"Cyrus, this may come as a surprise to you, but I've never even had an affair," Delle confessed.

"An affair. Is that what we almost had?" He laughed.

"Sex, then," she blurted. "Is that basic enough for you?" It was not a topic she felt comfortable discussing. Her mother had died before the subject had arisen, and Jeanette, after all these years, remained a stranger.

Cyrus laughed aloud, and Delle yanked her hand away as if she'd been stung. "You think it's funny? Dammit, Cyrus, how would you like to be a twenty-eight-year-old virgin? I can tell you, it's no laughing matter! Not even Hetty knows the truth, and the older I get, the more embarrassing it is."

He gave another shout of laughter and collapsed against the bulkhead, and after a moment, Delle subdued the urge to sock him and began to giggle. "All right, so now you know. If you ever—*ever*—dare tell a soul, I'll come back here and haunt you."

Turning, he gathered her in his arms, his shoulders still shaking. "Honey, you're going to haunt me anyway, but if it bothers you all that much, I'd be glad to offer my services."

"You're so generous." With her face buried in the damp warmth of his throat, she sniffed, giggled once more and then sighed. "Cyrus, what are we going to do?"

A good question, he repeated to himself. A damned good question.

Seven

"I didn't get around to telling you, but you had company this afternoon," Cyrus announced as they pulled into the driveway some half an hour later. They'd both grown increasingly silent on the short cruise in.

Chewing on a fingernail, something she had not done in twenty years, Delle was feeling the wobbliness that comes from having been on the water. The fact that she'd had to leave her car on the other side of the inlet overnight only added to her feelings of insecurity.

It took a moment for his words to register. "Company? But who could— Oh, good Lord, don't tell me my bachelor finally showed up."

Cyrus led the way to the house, opened the door and switched on a light. "Your what?"

"The one Hetty sent me, remember? Heaven only knows what she bribed this one with. Last time it was an introduction to a casting director at a Charlotte film studio. Once it was a season pass to the home games." She peeled off her jacket, tossed it across a chair and stroked the head of the decoy in passing. So far she'd avoided looking directly at Cyrus. "You can't imagine what that does for my ego year after year," she said dryly. "I'm beginning to feel like I ought to offer a rebate coupon if a man asks me out on a date."

Stifling a smile, Cyrus crossed to the corner where brown fungus sprouted discreetly between the boards. "Leave your ego to me, and don't be so quick to jump to conclusions." Raking a knuckle down a suspiciously dark crack, he said, "Your friends came by to see you this afternoon. The gulls."

"Are you serious? They came all the way back *here*?"

"They've been staying up at Kitty Hawk—on their way home now, ferry-hopping from Hatteras to here, to Ocracoke and then on to Cedar Island." He didn't add that after June Gavin's inquisition he was more than ever convinced that he was the candidate she'd had in mind all along. Evidently she considered his present life-style merely a passing phase, because there had been several rather pointed questions about his plans for returning to Charlotte.

Delle plopped herself down and planted her chin on her fists, blind date forgotten. "Well, damn!" she said plaintively. "And all this time they were only two islands away?" She felt betrayed. "Why would they lie to me? I could have joined them at Kitty Hawk. It's only a couple of hours away."

Tears of self-pity sprang into being, making her feel even worse. Her chin began to quiver, and she pressed it harder against her fists and hoped the brown fungus would continue to claim Cyrus's attention until she had herself under control again. All in all, it had not been one of her more memorable days.

By the time Cyrus gave up on the paneling and dropped down beside her on the couch, not a single tear had overflowed. Delle swallowed hard and widened her eyes, hoping to contain any remaining moisture.

"I'm sorry, Delle. I know you're disappointed, but—"

"I am not," she denied instantly. "I only agreed to come because I needed a rest, and I'd hardly have gotten one with those three clowns around. Actually, as things turned out, it's been a pretty good vacation." She peeped at him through tear-spangled lashes and glanced quickly away again. "Did they leave a message—a note?"

"The dark-haired one, Hetty, said something about calling you later."

"I've probably missed that, too," Delle said morosely.

"Look, why don't I fix us something to eat?" Cyrus suggested tactfully.

"I'm stuffed."

"To drink?"

She sighed. She wanted *something*; she just didn't know what. A pound of cashews? A huge box of chocolates? Even a stomachache would be better than this vague feeling of disillusionment. At least she'd know what to take for a stomachache. "Oh, how do I know what I want?" she growled. "Stop pressuring me, Cyrus."

Not by so much as the blink of an eye did he acknowledge the unfairness of her charge, thus adding guilt to her burden of woes.

"Oh, Cyrus, I'm sorry," Delle muttered. "It's just—oh, I don't know. Maybe I'm so used to pressure at work that I can't function without it."

"Doesn't sound too healthy."

"It's nothing a little planning and positive thinking won't straighten out," Delle dismissed, sorry she'd ever mentioned it. To think they'd been on the verge of making love less than an hour ago. God, this vacation had been a learn-

ing experience, if nothing else. As for Cyrus, he'd done little but bail her out ever since she'd arrived on this forsaken
sandpile. Small wonder she fancied herself in love with him.

With a gentle stroke of his thumb, Cyrus wiped the fur-
rows from between her brows. "Positive thinking is pretty
hard work. If you need a friendly shoulder to cry on, mine
are guaranteed waterproof."

Delle managed a watery smile. "Don't be so nice to me,
dammit—I already feel like a rag doll, and you're pulling my
stuffing out. A little more sympathy, and I'll never find the
strength to leave."

Did he stiffen, or was it only her imagination? When he
spoke, his deep drawl held the same rich blend of gentleness and humor. "I reckon we could all move over and make
room for one more person on the island. As long as you
don't gain any weight."

"Will you *stop that*?" She pinched his thigh, but then her
hand lingered on, drawing on the warm strength that was so
much a part of him. "Speaking of moving, I really need to
check in with Daniel—my secretary—and see what he's got
set up for next week. I could be in New York tomorrow
night, ready for a round of appointments Monday morning."

For a long time, Cyrus didn't speak. Then he said quietly, "Just my luck we had to meet when you were going up
the ladder and I was coming down."

A sound escaped Delle's lips—part laughter, part sob.
"You're clogging my sinuses again," she warned. Afraid to
meet his eyes, she stared at his hands, instead. He'd lifted
the battered decoy from the stack of magazines on the coffee table, and was caressing its scarred wooden back in slow,
rhythmic strokes. His hands were work-hardened, but
beautifully formed, and she remembered with a rush of heat
the way they'd felt on her body.

Unconsciously, she parted her lips as she watched his sensitive touch on the battered wood. Was it possible she'd known this man for less than a week? She felt as if she'd known him forever. Without thinking, she said, "Funny, isn't it? In spite of everything, I still feel more comfortable with you than with anyone I've ever known."

"Comfortable," Cyrus repeated thoughtfully. "Like an old shoe, you mean?"

"No, *not* like an old shoe." Her lips quivered into a reluctant grin. "The trouble with feeling comfortable is that you end up talking too much and then regretting it." The word "comfortable" didn't begin to describe her feelings toward Cyrus Burrus—and yet it was true as far as it went. "Look, could we just forget it?"

"You mean it's not true?"

"It's true, it's true! That is, *most* of the time it's true."

"But not *all* the time. Thank God for that, at least. I'd hate to think you were comfortable the whole time we were anchored outside the harbor. I know I sure as hell wasn't."

"Let it drop, Cyrus," Delle requested, not wanting to be reminded.

"No way, love. We still have some unfinished business, but I'm not sure this is the right time to go into it."

"There's no business to go into, finished or unfinished." A little wildly, she wondered what he'd say if she told him she was falling in love with him. It probably wasn't the first time he'd tried his hand with a tourist, nor would it be the last. One of the perks of island life, probably, but it hurt to think about it. It hurt badly.

One thing stood out clearly—there was no future for them together. The sooner she got away, the better her chances of recovery.

Cyrus's fingers curled into his palms. He could follow her thought processes as clearly as if she'd voiced every doubt. God knows, he'd lain awake long enough, trying to find the answers. If only they had more time, he told himself, hating the feeling of helplessness. "Do you really have to go to New York tomorrow, Delle?"

"I really do. It's the next logical step, Cyrus. It's time to move on, I've been in one place too long. Lately, I even dread getting out of bed—the sight of my own desk gives me a pain." She sighed, and his short nails bit into the tough calluses of his palms as he fought against frustration—against the fear of losing her before they'd even had a chance to explore this thing that was happening to them both.

And damn it, it *was* happening to them both—to her, too! He was almost certain of it, only why couldn't she see it? Why wouldn't she at least give them a chance?

"The logical move is to a bigger bank," she went on in a reasonable tone that drove him up the wall. "The next move will be to the largest bank in a smaller city. My New York experience will count for more there, and I'll be able to trade on it to a better advantage. That last was Oren's suggestion—I haven't had time to think about it yet."

Spoken aloud, it didn't sound quite so clever as when Oren had suggested it. In fact, Delle thought, unconsciously slipping off her shoes and lifting her feet up to the warm place beside Cyrus's body—it sounded hard-boiled and calculating.

But only, she told herself, because this was the wrong setting for mapping out her strategy. She leaned back against the cushions, savoring the warm and slightly shabby comfort of her surroundings. She'd miss this cottage. She'd miss Cyrus. Dear Lord, she couldn't bear to think about how much she was going to miss him!

"If that's what you want," he said quietly, "I wish you luck." Lifting her legs onto his lap, he cradled her feet in his hands and began massaging them with a sure, firm touch. "Cold feet, warm heart."

"Mmm, that's wonderful. Makes me feel all disconnected—especially my brain."

"I should have tried it sooner. Then maybe you'd put New York on hold and stay on here long enough to learn to cast properly. There's a drum out there with your name on it." He kept his voice carefully noncommittal, as if it were of small interest to him whether she stayed or not. The idea of luring her back aboard the boat and anchoring offshore until spring he dismissed as impractical.

"You're putting me to sleep," Delle purred. "I'm going to catch my fish one of these days—I don't give up that easily. But even if I wanted to stay on, Cyrus, I couldn't. The cottage was only rented for a week."

"I could arrange it. Oh, hell, honey, this place belongs to me. It's yours for as long as you want it."

Delle propped herself up on her elbows to stare at him. Was he serious? Did he think he had to impress her by claiming to own a house? "Cyrus..."

"For just a few days more. Delle, I don't want you to go." There, he'd gone halfway. He'd all but come out and told her how he felt. The next move was up to her.

As the silence stretched out to brittle dimensions, he dumped her feet and stood up. "I'll make coffee," he muttered, suddenly needing action.

Dammit, he could kill those three meddlesome witches for what they'd done to him. He'd been reasonably content with his life until *she'd* come barging out of the house at daybreak in her underwear! How could a man ask a woman to give up everything she'd worked for and join him in a self-imposed exile on an island where she'd have little or no opportunities for her own interests?

He escaped to the kitchen, and Delle, bereft, pulled the afghan off the back of the couch and spread it over her bare feet. Cyrus splashed water over the base of the coffee maker, swore under his breath and willed his hands to steadiness. He mopped up and refilled the glass pot.

"Peter was there," Delle said. "With Oren."

Cyrus managed to place the pot on the base without dumping it again. He clutched the edge of the cabinet with both hands and closed his eyes. *Just what he needed!* "So how was the grand reunion? Like one of those commercials where the couple bound toward each other through fields of tall weeds, like a couple of drunken kangaroos?"

"My, aren't we cynical! At least I don't despise him any longer. I think ... I think I feel sorry for him." It was true. She hadn't known it until she heard herself speak the words.

"At least we have that in common," Cyrus muttered, heating milk to add to her mug. He felt sorry for any man who'd been fool enough to lose her.

Waiting for the coffee to finish dripping, he did his best to come to terms with a no-win situation. He wanted her here—she wanted to go. He was more certain every minute that what she thought she wanted was all wrong for her, but how could he tell her so? He could just imagine her response to that little gem.

Like it or not, he had to let her go and hope that she discovered for herself that her future wasn't in some damned office fighting a paper war, but here with him.

He poured the coffee, switched off the pot and turned toward the living room. And stopped in his tracks. Her eyes were closed, her lashes fanning out in stark contrast to her pale cheeks. His hand trembled, endangering the coffee. God, she was so lovely! She had all the fragile strength of a small Giacometti figure he'd once owned—the surface patina of the bronze version, the vulnerability of the terra cotta original.

As he approached, her eyes fluttered open, and Cyrus schooled his own features to hide the pain of loss he was already beginning to experience.

"I hadn't seen him in six years—Peter, that is. Do you know what?" She smiled, her dark eyes soft and sleepy. "He forgave me."

"You mean you forgave him?"

"No, I mean *he* forgave *me*. The old double standard is alive and well." She lifted her mug, sipped cautiously and licked the milky moisture from her lips. "This stuff is beginning to grow on me. At least it doesn't burn holes in my stomach. If you ever need a testimonial, Dr. B., just let me know."

"All patched up and ready for the front lines again, huh?"

Delle smiled drowsily, and Cyrus took his place beside her, shifting her feet back onto his lap. "At this rate, you're going to have to pour me into bed. I'm not sure I can make it under my own steam," she murmured.

The hand on her ankle tightened, and Cyrus, his voice sounding slightly strained, said, "Glad to oblige. That wouldn't be an invitation, would it?" At her quick look, he sighed. "No, I thought not. Drink up, honey. If I have to pour you into bed, we'd better get on with it, because I've got a net to fish before breakfast tomorrow."

"Just cover me up and blow out the candle on your way out."

"Trusting little thing, aren't you?"

"Where you're concerned," she admitted candidly. "You know, that's sort of ironic, isn't it? I mean, considering our shipboard romance and all."

"The romance that didn't quite come off." Oddly enough, joking about it wasn't as painful as he'd feared.

"Even if it had, I think I'd still feel the same way. Safe, I mean."

Cyrus winced, his fingers tightening on the ball of her right foot. "I'm not sure I'm flattered. Safe doesn't sound too exciting."

"Oh, you want excitement? Try corporate banking. Try competing with a school of barracudas in button-down shirts every day, and you'll get your excitement. You'll also get holes in your stomach."

"Ever consider getting out?"

As if she hadn't even heard him, Delle went on. "The higher I go at work, the fewer openings there are, and the tougher the competition for the best ones. Sometimes I think I should switch from wearing business suits to wearing a flak jacket."

"Is it worth it?"

She flung him a puzzled look. "Well, of course it's worth it. It's what I *do*," she explained, as if that said it all.

"Then I'm glad we're not in competition. I'd hate to stand between you and the fulfillment of your dreams."

Delle withdrew her foot from his lap and sat up. "I wasn't implying any criticism of your life-style, Cyrus. You're obviously happy here." Which was true. Nor did she respect him any less because he'd chosen not to compete in the real world. Some men were cut out for it, some weren't.

"I could be more content, Delle," he ventured.

He didn't have to elaborate. The deeper note in his voice was enough to trigger her defenses. "What time is it? You've got a net to fish and I have a ferry to catch," she reminded him, placing her unfinished coffee on the table.

"So that's it, huh?" he said, the bitter inflection taking her by surprise.

"Cyrus, you're not going to start anything, are you?"

Standing abruptly, he began to prowl, ending up staring out the window into the pitch-dark night. The stars were no longer visible.

Delle watched helplessly, wanting to go to him, knowing it would be fatal. He should never have come inside with her. He should never have gone to Hatteras to bring her back—she should never have come here in the first place, but oh, Lord, she was glad she had. Glad, even if she never got over him.

He turned away from the window, his eyes looking more black than green. "Delle, I don't want you to go, not like this. We need more time together."

She crumpled. "Cyrus, don't," she whispered.

"Dammit, don't hide your head in the sand! I think you know how I feel. God knows, I've tried to talk myself out of it, but it's no good."

"That's right, Cyrus, it's no good. Whatever it is— whatever we feel for each other, it can't be real. It's too soon." She uttered a short laugh that failed miserably. "Look at what happened with Peter. I'd known him all my life, and I nearly made a horrible mistake."

"I'm not Peter," he said with a quiet dignity that brought an ache to her throat. *Delle, I love you, but how can I tell you? How can I ask you to throw away everything you think you want and take me, instead?*

He couldn't ask—he couldn't even risk telling her, for the asking was implicit in the telling. And she was right, it was too soon. Only he'd never been more sure of anything in his life.

And then she was on her feet. Later, Cyrus never knew which one of them made the first move. All he knew was that she was in his arms, clinging, crying. He aimed a kiss at her lips and missed, catching her somewhere on the side of the nose, and that was wonderful, too. He wanted to kiss every inch of her, to love every wonderful part of her, to give her something to take away with her, if go she must.

"Delle—" he said hoarsely, his lips buried in her throat as he led her toward the bedroom.

"Don't say anything, Cyrus. None of this makes sense, and I don't want to think about it. Just love me."

Still holding her, he reached out to switch on the bedside lamp, and Delle shook her head. "Please—I don't want the light."

"No talking, no looking, no thinking, is that it?" The note of humor was as ragged as torn velvet.

"Please," she whispered. "Just hold me."

Her blouse came off first, and then Cyrus's shirt. By the time he reached for the button at the waist of her slacks, Delle's vision had adjusted to the dim light that spilled through the doorway. Her eyes devoured the beauty of his strong, uneven features, her hands already laying claim to the broad wall of his chest.

A few ounces of raw silk slithered down her bare legs and she kicked it aside, feeling proud, shy—wondering if he was disappointed in her. "Cyrus, I—"

"What, sweetheart?" The words were murmured against her lips as he drew her naked body back into his arms. He was still wearing his jeans—soft, faded to the color of a summer sky, worn low on his hips.

He stood still as she explored the breadth of his chest, the swirling pattern of dark hair that encircled his masculine nipples before narrowing downward. Her fingertips found the peaks, lingered, brushing back and forth as he hardened under her touch, then feathered down his middle to the snap on his jeans. "Nothing," she said faintly.

A film of moisture suddenly beaded his face as he fought for control. How could any woman so obviously made for love have escaped it all these years? He had no doubt that she'd been telling him the truth on that score. She'd been embarrassed to admit it, as though it made her slightly less than desirable. He was no saint, and God knows, he didn't equate celibacy with morality, but all the same, the incredible knowledge that no man had ever known the warm secret places of her body aroused in him a primordial need that shook him to the depths of his very soul.

"Are you cold?" Delle asked. She wasn't. Her skin was burning feverishly.

"Do I feel cold to you?"

"I thought maybe—your jeans? I'm beginning to feel a little bit underdressed."

It took less than a moment to even the score, and then he lowered her onto the bed, filling his eyes with her loveliness. In the dim yellow glow, her body was all shadowy contours and warm highlights. Before this night was over, Cyrus determined to burn his brand on every tender inch of her body, claiming her for his so that there'd be no doubt in her mind when she left there.

She *had* to come back to him. But it had to be her own decision.

Delle felt a throbbing heat spread through her as she studied his body openly. A museum-goer all her life, she'd seen the male torso interpreted in both bronze and marble. The living flesh was another thing altogether. He was still deeply tanned, all but a narrow band about his hips. As if drawn by its paleness, her eyes moved downward over his midriff. And widened.

Cyrus, sensitive to her unspoken fears, took her hand and placed it over his heart. "Feel that?" he whispered. "You're better than aerobics."

"You, too," she breathed, her voice as thin as vapor. "I— Cyrus, I'm not exactly—"

"Prepared?" Cursing his lack of foresight, he fought for a semblance of calmness. "I'm not either, darling, but I can still make it happen for you." *And die a martyr's death.*

"Oh, no," she said hurriedly, both touched and embarrassed. "I—it's the safest time for me. I've read the books. I'm just not—that is, I don't..." She knew the facts; what she didn't know was how to deal with this deep, sweet ache that was driving her frantic. She wanted him—she *needed* him desperately, but he seemed perfectly content to lie there and look at her. "Isn't it—aren't you...supposed to kiss me now? Or something?"

With a harsh groan, he caught her to him, rolling over until he was half covering her with his body. "I didn't want to rush you, darling. I can wait if you still have any doubts." *Sure he could. And she could sweep up his ashes tomorrow and dump them into the sea!*

If Delle had had any doubts at all, they were lost when his mouth came down on hers, hungrily taking his fill of all she had to offer and seeking more. Demanding more. After a while, his hands began to move over her body, and this time he demanded nothing, rather letting her needs direct his touch. She shifted her shoulders restlessly, and he claimed a breast, stroking the already taut peak until she whimpered against his mouth.

As his lips moved down to take possession of the tender prize, his hands journeyed slowly downward, exploring the delicate curve of her hips, the faint swell of her abdomen. His fingertips brushed the edges of the thatch of tangled silk before sliding gently between her thighs. Delle gasped and then moaned softly. She began to move in unconscious harmony with his caresses.

All too soon, every atom of her being was focused on a small triangle in the center of her body, and he was doing things that made her want to cry, want to shout. Bands of pleasure began to gather about her, drawing closer, closer. From somewhere nearby she heard the plaintive cry of a night bird—no, the sound of a woman's voice. Hers?

"Please, Cyrus, please, Cyrus, please," she whimpered over and over, seeking deliverance. Her hips lifted of their own volition, and he slipped his hands beneath her and moved carefully between her thighs.

Slowly, ever mindful of the need for gentleness, he knelt at the door of her womanhood and then slipped into its heated embrace, shuddering under the bonds of self-imposed restraint.

Delle, her breath coming in shallow little gasps, tensed as she felt him begin to fill her, and he stopped instantly. Above her his face was harsh and strained—for a moment, the face of a stranger. She closed her eyes, and gradually she relaxed.

The pleasure circles quickly surrounded her again, moving closer, glowing, wavering—never coming quite close enough to touch. Frantically, she began to move. Her hands at first, lifting to flutter over the sharp-etched angle of his cheeks, and then gripping his shoulder. She lifted her hips, wanting more of him, not knowing how to tell him.

"I won't hurt you, love—I'll never hurt you," he whispered.

"Oh, Cy, I don't know if I can bear this. I'm melting, something's happening.... *Please*," she wailed.

"It's all right, Delle, it's all right—trust me. Let go, sweetheart, don't hold back anything."

Her thighs tightened about his hips, and he began to thrust, stroke by slow, powerful stroke, building the tension until both their bodies were bathed in sweat. He felt her abdomen quiver against his, felt the trembling begin deep inside her as she clasped him convulsively, and he cried her name twice as he hurtled into space.

"Are you all right, love?" he panted a long time later, after the wild, exhalted journey had ended and he was back on earth once more.

"Sleepy. A li'l nap first, but then..."

"Hmm?"

"More, please?"

Squeezing her to him, Cyrus laughed softly. He was winded, exhausted, and he'd never felt more wonderful in his life. Delle was already asleep in his arms, her hair strewn across his face, and he breathed its fragrance, smiling into the darkness.

The smile faded, though. He lay for a long time, holding her, listening to the soft whisper of her breathing as he stared up at the faint watermarks on the ceiling.

Sometime during the night, Delle shivered. It had grown cold, but as they'd been lying on top of the covers, there hadn't been a whole lot Cyrus could do about it, short of waking her up. His head had told him to get up and locate a blanket; his heart had whispered that between the furnace and his body heat, he could keep her warm a little while longer.

The truth was, he was scared stiff. After tonight, she could hardly walk away as if nothing had changed between them. On the other hand, he was still faced with the same old dilemma; he could ask her to resign her position and let him make a life for her here, but dare he risk it?

He was as certain as he'd ever been of anything in his life that she wasn't cut out for the path she was determined to follow. He'd been that route. Changing his whole life-style hadn't been easy; not a single friend had backed up his decision. They'd all thought he was crazy to throw away a life-style that most men only dreamed about, but even before the vandalism, his life had begun to ring hollow. It had taken weeks to work his way through that particular trauma, but he'd come out the other side with a much clearer vision of what he wanted out of life. It couldn't be found in the places where he'd been looking, but he'd known instinctively where to go. His father had left him property on Coranoke. He'd loved the island since he'd left it as a child after his parents' divorce.

All right, so he'd simplified his life, honed it to the basics. He had all the security a man could hope for in this life, plus the satisfaction of being able to make a small contribution.

He was free to do the things he wanted to do, to build, to plant, to fish—to follow the tradition of his forebearers.

But what did Delle know of this kind of life? Did he have a right to make the decision for her? At this point, she might even agree, but it had to be a rational decision, not an emotional one.

He'd give her time, and then, if she came to him of her own free will, they could go from there. The next step had to be hers, though, and the knowledge that she might not take that step was killing him.

Eight

It was late when Delle awoke. For a long time she just lay there, eyes closed, feeling the way she'd felt when, at seven, she'd climbed a ladder someone had left propped against an apple tree, determined to reach the fruit that dangled beguilingly out of reach on the very tip of one of the higher branches. She'd almost made it when the branch began to sag under her slight weight. Petrified, she'd shut her eyes and forced herself to creep backward until her bottom bumped against the main trunk. Somehow, she'd managed to get herself turned around, and there she'd remained, stomach threatening rebellion, arms clinging tightly to the rough bark, until she was rescued by the gardener.

She felt precisely the same way now. Only this time, there was no one to pluck her back to safety. It was up to her to get herself back down to earth, and the longer she waited, the harder it was going to be.

"It's time," she whispered. "Past time." She knew without having to look that Cyrus was gone. He'd left without even waking her to say goodbye. All right, so the bed was narrow. There wasn't a double bed in the cottage, only twins, but she hadn't heard him complaining about the crowded conditions last night.

But it wasn't that, and Delle knew it. Cyrus's sense of self-preservation was evidently more fully developed than her own.

Memories began to sprout like tiny seedlings, and ruthlessly, she yanked them out and tossed them aside. All right, so it had happened. It had been inevitable, she supposed, and someday she'd be able to think about it objectively, but not now. *Definitely* not now!

The tiny green room with its white rugs and white café curtains looked gray and uninviting. It was raining again, in spite of the promise of last night's stars. Liquid sunshine.

Delle was perversely glad of the dismal weather. It was in keeping with her mood. It would make it a lot easier to leave this island, and once away from here, once back where she belonged, she could start putting the pieces together again. She was good at that.

Not bothering to dress first, she began throwing things into her bag. The suitcase crammed full, she sat on it and snapped the lock. Then, with a soft oath, she opened it again and took out a pair of slacks that were only slightly rumpled, a set of underwear and her turtleneck sweater. "Very efficient," she muttered under her breath as she turned on the water in the shower. At this rate, she'd make a terrific impression in New York.

Hot water sent billowing steam to cloud the bathroom mirror, and Delle swore softly. *Now* he got around to fixing the blasted heater!

Not long afterward, she slammed the front door behind her, prepared to dash out to her car and sling her suitcase into the back. "Oh, hell and damnation," she cried. She'd forgotten that it was pouring, and that her car was at Hatteras. "No wonder this place never made it as a resort. Nothing works right, from the ferries to the blasted weather!"

On the autumn schedule, there were only four ferries a day leaving for Hatteras. They left this side on the hour, and if she missed the first one she'd have to wait until eleven. That meant school-bus traffic, or rush-hour traffic on the other end—or both. Plus the rain. She just didn't think she could cope with that today.

She had approximately seven minutes to get herself and her luggage to the ferry. If she walked, she'd never make it in time. Besides, she'd drown before she got there, but it was either that or call Cyrus to rescue her again. She'd swim the inlet first.

The note was beside the coffee maker, where he'd known she'd eventually find it. Delle stared blindly at the bold pattern of vertical strokes and neatly formed loops, and then wadded it up unread and tossed it into the trash. She didn't want to know what his excuse was. She didn't want to think about last night, not until she was safely off this miserable island, where thinking couldn't get her into more trouble than she was already in.

With three hours to kill, she made coffee and rummaged among the paperbacks until she found a gory-looking mystery. She'd take a cue from Cyrus's grandmother and do absolutely nothing until it slacked off. If it didn't, she'd wrap both herself and her suitcase in plastic trash bags, roll up her pants and wade. One way or another, she was going to catch that next ferry.

Eleven came and went. By noon there was still no sign of a let-up. The rain came down in solid gray sheets, driven by a fierce northeast wind. Delle was frustrated, worried and hungry. Every minute she remained there increased the chance of seeing Cyrus again, and she wasn't ready for that. She might never be ready.

At least a dozen times she reached for the crumpled piece of paper in the trash can, tempted to smooth it out and see what his excuse had been, but her nerve always failed at the last moment.

Probably something original like, "It's been nice knowing you." Or worse—"Thanks for the fun evening. C. B."

"That wretch!"

The painful gnawing of her stomach finally drove her into the kitchen, where she reluctantly took down a can of soup, its ends speckled with rust, the label peeling up at the seam. The first can she'd tried had hardly been palatable, but it was either that or shriveled green onions, stale crackers and assorted condiments.

Even the search for a pan to heat it in brought back memories. Hiding her purse in the double boiler and being rescued by Cyrus a short time later. A copper stock pot filled with Cyrus's delectable seafood bisque...

Delle tried to tell herself it was all a game with him, a game he played each summer when the beaches swarmed with vacationers, but somehow, the picture refused to come into focus.

It was mostly her fault—that romantic schoolgirl imagination she thought she'd outgrown. She'd let herself get carried away. But then, Cyrus obviously had lots of practice charming lady tourists; he did it so skillfully. She'd been no match for him.

She struggled with the can opener. It, too, was slightly rusted. Where *was* that overgrown Boy Scout when she needed him? She refused to call for help, but dammit, he might have had the common courtesy to check on her welfare. After all, it was his island, and she was still a guest here.

"I'll report him to the chamber of commerce," she threatened, finally managing to get the lid off the can of split pea soup.

She'd just managed to scoop the last of the sickly green contents into a pan when the phone rang. "About time," she muttered. Studying the knobs until she located the right front, she turned it on high. He'd have some slick excuse about fishing his net or crabbing his pot or whatever, and she didn't want to hear it.

On the eighth ring, she snatched it up and barked a greeting.

"Well! Thought for a minute there you'd flown the coop," Hetty drawled.

"Hetty? Where on earth are you? Fine friends you three turned out to be!"

"We thought so," Hetty replied smugly. "How'd you like him?"

"Him who?"

"Don't be dense, Cordelia. Why do you think June got a convenient toothache? We wanted to leave the coast clear for you two."

"The blasted coast hasn't been clear since I rolled off the ferry. Everything I own is wet and beginning to smell like mildew."

"Cozy, huh? An open fire, a jug of wine and thou?"

"At the moment, I'd trade both thou and the fire for a loaf of fresh bread. Did you know that there's not a single restaurant on this whole island? If you want a decent meal, you have to go to Ocracoke or Hatteras, and since the last ferry leaves both islands at five-thirty, you're stuck."

"By the time we approach thirty, most of us have learned how to cook, believe it or not. You're the only woman I know who can ruin instant grits."

"*Some* of us have more interesting things to do," Delle said defensively.

"I told you I'd be back." He reached for her, and for a moment she resisted, but then she crumpled against him, hiding in the warmth of his strong arms. "Oh, hell, honey, I was afraid. Things have moved so fast between us—I thought if I got away from you for a little while, maybe I could work out something."

"And did you?" she whispered.

He shook his head. "Same old impasse. Damned if I do and damned if I don't. If you want to know the shameful truth, I knew you couldn't get away in this rain, not without your car. I've been watching the cottage before every ferry, though, and if you'd set out on foot, I'd have kidnapped you and kept you here if I'd had to sit on you."

A whimper of laughter escaped her. She lifted her face, and that was a mistake. Cyrus claimed her lips with a fierceness born of need and doubts and desperation.

Like lightning in dry grass, the passion sparked, quickly flaring out of control. There was no gentleness in the bruising pressure of his lips, the thrust of his tongue, as if by the sheer violence of his kiss, he sought to ease the pain that rode him so relentlessly.

It was no good. His masculine strength was no match for the beguiling softness of her, the sweet, feminine scent of her skin. He cradled her in his arms and swayed with her, raining kisses over her swollen lips, her cheeks, in the vulnerable hollow just under her chin.

"Stay with me, love," he murmured, leading her toward the bedroom, where her suitcase was packed and ready to go. "I need you."

No, please, Delle begged silently. *Don't ask for more than I can give.* Her fingers trembled at the buttons of his shirt, craving the feel of the hard, warm body whose wonders she'd only begun to discover. "I need you, too, Cyrus," she whispered. "I'm so glad you came back before—"

"You're going, then?" He stood before her, his eyes strangely dark as they searched her face. His breathing was ragged, and Delle knew he wanted her. She prayed that he was as powerless as she was to resist this fierce, irresistible compulsion. Just once more, let him make her body sing, let *her* bring that same sweet magic to *him*, and she'd forgive him for allowing her to fall in love.

"Don't talk. Just make love to me, Cyrus." She laid his shirt open and lifted her hands to his body, tracing the patterns of body hair that accentuated the swell of his masculine chest as they swirled around his dark nipples and dived toward the low, beltless waist of his jeans.

"No looking, no talking," he teased, leading her over to the bed. "Bankers always impose too many rules." As her fingers strayed down his stomach to toy with the snap at the top of his zipper, he shuddered. The hard slab of his abdomen jerked against her knuckles.

Delle's confidence grew at the visible evidence of her effect on him. Once more; was that too much to ask? It would have to last her a long, long time, for she knew she couldn't come back—once she left the island, she'd never find the courage to return, in case another woman was installed in the cottage—in her place.

"Undress me, love?" Cyrus had himself under control now. Barely. If this was the way she wanted to play it, he'd go along. God, he didn't have a whole lot of choice. She'd all but paralyzed him when she'd taken the initiative that way. His Delle—his shy, courageous, funny, brilliant Delle. "I've never been undressed by a bank executive before," he confessed, eyes dancing with shards of green laughter. "Last night, I think both our clothes sort of self-destructed."

"Oh; we can do anything," Delle assured him, her arms sliding over his chest and out his shoulders to peel the shirt from his back. "Just as long as we don't have to read instructions."

"I have a feeling you're an atypical bank executive," Cyrus murmured, trailing his fingertips down over the evidence of her arousal. Through the soft knit, her nipples stood out clearly.

"Probably," Delle said breathlessly. For now, the bank was a million miles away. This was the only reality, the only thing in the whole world she wanted. Cyrus. His love, his passion, his gentleness.

Swaying beside the bed, she caressed every inch of his chest and his back, tasted the salt-sweet tang of his flesh with teeth and tongue. He stiffened and groaned, but he kept his hands at his sides. It was only when she steeled herself to take the next logical step, her hesitant fingertips straying back to the snap fastener of his jeans for perhaps the third time, that his control finally broke.

"My turn now, love," he said in a voice that was barely recognizable. His hands closed over her hips and slipped under the hem of her sweater, drawing it up over her shoulders. "Either that, or I take time out for a cold shower and then we begin all over again."

With her sweater momentarily covering her face, Delle was in no position to offer an opinion. Nor was she interested in cold showers. Especially not when her vision cleared to find Cyrus devouring her body with his eyes. Her breasts rose and fell with each deep, shuddering breath, quivering in rhythm with her pounding heart. Watery gray daylight spilled through the windows, and she didn't care. She wanted him to look at her, wanted him to find her beautiful, but at the same time, she couldn't help wondering if he was comparing her to all the other women he'd known.

At least he had no worries on that score. He was her first. He'd probably be her last. She couldn't conceive of sharing this intimacy with another man, of knowing this wild ecstasy with someone else. Her gaze dropped to where the jeans hugged his narrow hips, and she swallowed hard and closed her eyes. The sound of his soft laughter brought them open wide.

"You're a constant wonder, darling. Bold as a tiger one minute, shy as a doe the next." His hands slipped behind her hips, and he drew her against his taut masculine contours, touching her parted lips with dozens of small nibbling kisses while he caressed her with his body.

Delle tugged ineffectually at his jeans, devastated by a hunger that stripped away the last of her self-control. "Cyrus, help me," she whispered fiercely.

"Patience, love, patience. Don't be so impetuous." Brushing his teasing smile across her lips, he slowly removed the last scrap of her clothing, then he held her away from him. "Oh, Delle," he whispered reverently, "nothing this lovely was meant to be hidden under a pin-striped suit."

"How did you know—about my pin-striped suit?" Her voice broke as his lips closed over one nipple. His tongue explored the sensitive nugget until her knees sagged. "Cyrus, please—I can't take much more."

They tumbled onto the bed. Cyrus's body covered hers, pressing her deeply into the mattress until, with a low groan, he rolled off to one side. Taking her hand, he placed it on the heated skin just below his waist. "Care to have another go at that fastener?" he challenged.

Her trembling fingers slipped lower. She found the corroded brass snap and finally worked it free. Then, with thumb and forefinger, she lifted the tab of his zipper and began working it downward.

Cyrus stiffened, the sound of his indrawn breath like torn velvet. "Honey—" he gasped. "You might be able to handle this much stress, but I'm not as young as I used to be, and neither are these jeans." His breath coming in deep gasps, he removed her hands and a moment later, the last remaining barrier between them.

Delle was aching with need, molten with the sweet throb of desire that demanded fulfillment, and this time there was no reason for Cyrus to go slowly. "Please," she implored, pressing her body to his.

"You're sure? Oh, sweetheart—" There was a gleam of perspiration on the side of his face, on the satiny surface of his heavily muscled shoulder. His eyes moved over her face, as if committing it to memory.

Suffused with emotion, Delle felt her eyes brim. She wanted to wrap herself around him, to enclose him and never let him go. "Please," she repeated simply.

"At least this time I came prepared. Are you—all right? I mean, are you sore or anything?"

She didn't pretend not to understand. Nor was she embarrassed. "Slightly, but it's perfectly natural according to the instruction books." Her lips trembled as she hovered between laughter and tears.

He laughed softly. Taking her face in his hands, he traced the pure lines of her jaw, the slight hollow beneath her cheekbones with his lips. "Thought you didn't read instructions."

"There were plenty of pictures. As a photographer, I was interested enough in those to read the captions."

The shared laughter broke off as Delle's breath caught in her throat. Cyrus's lips moved to her breasts, suckling, caressing, while his hands ventured forth over the gentle terrain of her body. When his lips followed the course set by his seeking hands, she was swiftly engulfed in flames. Over and over she cried for release. Again and again he took her to the edge with kisses that had her clutching helplessly at his shoulders. She was too weak to utter a protest when he turned away, and before she could gather her strength, he was back again, lifting himself above her as he sought the ultimate intimacy.

Eyes closed tightly, every iron-hard muscle clenched in a shuddering attempt to stem the flow, Cyrus once more gave her time to adjust to his invasion. Never had he been more aware of the wondrous vulnerability of a woman's body.

Never had he been more aware of the vulnerability of a man with the woman he loved.

Cautiously, he deepened his thrust and began the slow movements that soon had Delle thrashing helplessly against the avalanche of sensation that was sweeping her over the precipice, into a world of exquisite pleasure.

"Cyrus, please—oh, no...ah, yes," she murmured brokenly as he lost control and began to drive urgently toward his own fulfillment.

"Yes, yes," she whispered light-years later when, still caught up in a blinding cosmic explosion, she felt him collapse over her body.

He kissed her lips, her eyes, her ears. Even now, she thought with the small part of her mind that was still functioning, he was loving. Without releasing her, he adjusted his weight, and she closed her eyes and allowed herself to drift. Just for a moment.

She must have slept. Much later, she remembered waking in Cyrus's arms, hearing him whisper love words.

Or perhaps she'd only dreamed the love words. The next time she opened her eyes, the coppery rays of sunset were beaming through the window. No rain, not a cloud in sight. "What time is it?" she mumbled, peering at her watch.

"What difference does it make?" Cyrus said sleepily from beside her.

Delle twisted her head around to stare at him. "What difference does it make? If it's after five, it means I'm stuck here for another night."

He rolled out of bed, stark naked, the glow filtering through the curtains turning his body orange. The stream of profanity that escaped him bore little resemblance to the tender words he'd uttered a short while ago.

"Are you always so sweet when you wake up?" Delle asked.

"Only when I wake up with a stubborn woman who can't see the truth when it hits her in the face."

"Oh? And does it happen often? Waking up with a woman, I mean."

Without bothering to answer, he stalked across the room to the bathroom, slamming the door behind him. A moment later the door opened, and he crossed the room to grab up her suitcase and returned to the bathroom again. "I'm going to shower," he said tersely. "You'd damned well better be here when I get out."

Delle was still where he'd left her when he emerged some five minutes later. "That was fast," she remarked.

"I wasn't inclined to linger."

"In other words, you didn't trust me."

"You catch on fast."

"May I have my suitcase now?" she said with excessive politeness. "I'd like to have a bath and get dressed and see if I can hire somebody to take me to Hatteras."

"Why?" he demanded bluntly. Delle wished, not for the first time, that he'd put on some clothes. He must know the effect his body had on women—he flaunted it often enough.

"What do you mean, why? I told you I was leaving, and you deliberately timed this little episode to make me miss the last ferry."

He turned away, but not before she'd seen the look of pain in his eyes.

"All right, so maybe you didn't do it deliberately," she relented. Dear Lord, why was she acting this way? Why couldn't she make herself stop? Because she was afraid she was mortally wounded and she wanted him to hurt, too?

"Thanks a whole lot," Cyrus snarled.

"But the effect is the same," she went on relentlessly. "Would you please put some clothes on?" she yelled. "It worked! You can chalk up one more lady tourist." Aghast, Delle heard the bitter words pouring from her lips. He didn't deserve that. She was as much to blame as he was—but she was so afraid. So desperately afraid that no matter what she did now, it would be the wrong move and she'd end up ruining her life.

The silence was explosive. After a hundred years or so, a branch scraped noisily against the eaves, and Cyrus shook his head. He picked up his jeans and stepped in them, sucking in his breath to zip them up, and Delle, to her everlasting shame, watched his every move. Her chest felt as if someone had dumped a load of bricks on it, her throat ached and her eyes burned unbearably.

"I'll arrange for Cromer Williams to run you across the inlet. Be ready in half an hour."

Delle got out of bed, dragging the sheet around her. For the sake of her pride, which was about all she had left, she was determined not to let him have the last word. "Wait until I get my purse, will you Cyrus? I suppose the rent on this place has already been taken care of, but I still owe you gas money for picking me up at the marina yesterday. As for your time—"

He told her what she could do with her money just before he jerked open the front door and disappeared.

"Oh, God," Delle whispered brokenly, dropping onto the nearest chair. How could she have been so awful? How could *he* have been so impossible?

But in all fairness, what else could he have done? she asked herself. If her pride had been macerated, his couldn't be in much better shape. She'd done a pretty thorough job on him.

A chip off the old block, Oren had called her. He didn't know how right he was. Cordell Richardson to a T. Oh, her father was great as long as he had half an acre of mahogany desk in front of him, but in close quarters, on a one-to-one basis, he was a total write-off.

And she was no better.

Nine

It was years since Delle had been to New York. During her college years she'd spent summers abroad. She'd also done her junior year in Paris, facts that she'd summed up in her resumé as an "international perspective." Thanksgivings she'd spent in New York while her father and brothers flew to a hunt club somewhere out west. Her father considered shopping in New York the feminine equivalent of trophy hunting, and using his credit cards for ammunition, she'd dutifully bagged her limit.

Now she flinched at the blare of horns and the screech of brakes as her cabdriver won another bluff on his way from the airport to the hotel. Traffic in Norfolk was bad enough, but it couldn't begin to compare with the frenetic energy of New York City. The week's hibernation at Coranoke hadn't helped. Delle felt as if she'd been dropped in the middle of an enormous anthill, an alien species in danger of being trampled underfoot, if not actually eaten alive.

With his usual thoughtfulness, Daniel had scheduled her interviews to allow time between each one for her to assimilate and file away facts and impressions before going on to the next. Bless his foresightedness, she thought as she climbed into another taxi the following morning. Her reflexes were still geared down to Coranoke's speed.

It didn't help matters that she couldn't seem to generate any real enthusiasm for what she was about to undertake. Her body went through the motions, but her mind was somewhere else.

Cyrus. What was he doing now? Mending the roof over some other unsuspecting woman's head? Fixing her breakfast?

A spear of pain lanced through her, and she uttered a soft oath. "Not now," she muttered, and then flushed as the cabbie's head tilted inquiringly. "Uh—I said, nice day," she covered. It was raining. Cyrus had ruined her for rainy days.

After a night spent lying awake, listening to the sounds of the city and trying not to think about him, she'd finally got up, called room service for coffee and run herself a deep bath. Even hot water reminded her of Cyrus.

She arrived at her first appointment five minutes early. Some twenty minutes later she was shown into a cramped office, where a stick-figure man in a black suit continued to shuffle papers for several moments before looking at her over the top of his black-rimmed glasses.

H. Horace Henderson's greeting consisted of a single nod and a gesture to be seated. "Cordelia Richardson, Norfolk Trust and Fidelity, ten o'clock, November twentieth," he rattled off.

Delle glanced pointedly at the chunk of onyx on his desk that incorporated two penholders and a digital clock. It was now nineteen past the hour.

"Well, you're here now, that's the bottom line," Henderson stated grudgingly. "I have another appointment at ten-thirty so shall we begin?"

Delle almost strangled. She managed to nod.

"We do things differently here in New York, Miss Richardson. Your being a woman is entirely irrelevant."

To you, maybe—not to me, Delle fumed, missing part of his next statement.

"—where you're from or what you look like. It's the business that counts in the city, Miss Richardson. That's the bottom line."

If he "bottom-lined" her one more time, she was going to crown him with his damned desk set!

"Cooler heads prevail here in New York. People want the best deal available, and they'll do business wherever they get it."

"My resumé—" Delle began, and he cut her off.

"I have it on file. Now, you realize, Miss Richardson, that if we do decide to hire you—"

To *hire* her! To hire her? She wasn't some high school graduate applying for a job as a cashier, for goodness sake.

"—understand, of course, that banks have more vice presidents than they do tellers," Henderson pointed out.

Which meant that he was not going to offer her enough to live on, Delle interpreted. She uncrossed her ankles and prepared to rise. "Actually, my own bank is considering opening a loan office here in New York. I haven't yet made up my mind whether or not to accept the post of senior vice president in charge of commercial and retail banking."

He gave her a skeptical look, as well he should. If she thought she'd had the chance of a snowball, she wouldn't be wasting her time here. N. T. and F. moved at a snail's pace, and if New York figured in their plans at all, Delle would be the last one to get the nod.

"Thank you for your time, Mr. Henderson," she said graciously. *May you trip on your bottom line and break your scrawny little neck!*

The next appointment went much better. She was treated to coffee and a Danish, as her interviewer had not got around to having breakfast. Unfortunately, the position Delle was interested in had already been filled. Mrs. Kolodny apologized for not having notified her in time.

While Delle rested her feet, which resented being forced back into city shoes, they munched, sipped and discussed a critically acclaimed Broadway show that Delle had missed, and the new fall fashions, in which she was not particularly interested. She left feeling that perhaps she could handle New York after all.

But by the time she called room service and ordered her dinner, Delle admitted to herself that she wasn't even going to try. She got out the itinerary Daniel had prepared for her and left it by the phone. First thing in the morning she'd call and cancel the rest of her interviews.

What was the point of pretending any longer? Six years ago she might have been able to do it. Six years ago she'd had the energy and the determination to pin her sights on a single goal and not let up until she'd achieved it. It had been like swimming against the current at the best of times, like climbing a mountain in the face of an avalanche at worst, but she'd done it. Her own family had provided her with the motivation, and anger had provided the drive. Once under way, she'd never looked back.

In the beginning, she'd lacked the experience even to envision her final goal. Now that she had the experience she needed for the next big step in her career plan, she found that she lacked the drive. No longer angry over something that had happened so long ago, she'd exhausted her supply of energy.

Munching butterfly shrimp, Delle sat cross-legged in the middle of her king-size bed and tried to sort things out. What now? Go back to Norfolk and resume her place in the rat race? Everyone would know. Daniel was a wonderful secretary, but he had his faults, gossip being among them. Ten to one he'd already let drop a few hints about moving with her to New York, and by now the whole building would be buzzing with speculation.

What would Oren say when she told him she'd given up before she'd even begun?

Who *cared* what Oren thought?

"Dammit, Cyrus, this is your fault!" In less than a week, the man had managed to undermine her whole life. "Cyrus," she whispered, staring down at a half-eaten fan of butterfly shrimp. "What am I supposed to do now?"

Using three fingers, Cyrus typed the address on the last envelope and slipped the letter inside. One more chore off the list. He liked to stay in fairly close contact with his counselors over the winter, keeping them apprised of developments. They were all excellent, caring young people who were preparing for careers in social service, and Camp Reliance was a valuable experience for them. A part of the state-sanctioned Therapeutic Wilderness Program, it served as an alternative to juvenile institutions for boys with behavioral problems or those who were in trouble with the law for the first time.

Cyrus's boys were carefully screened. His facilities were much more limited than those of the other four wilderness camps in the system, and unlike the others, operated only during the summer months. Before he'd ever started, he'd held meetings with the other villagers, letting them know exactly what he wanted to do, and why. He hadn't pulled his punches. The boys he intended to bring to the island all had a history of trouble—truancy, petty theft, aggressive behavior. They were children with low self-esteem, those from problem homes, or no homes at all. Often they were runaways who, for one reason or another, couldn't go back, but who weren't ready to be fostered.

To their credit, not one of the villagers opposed him. Cyrus owned the largest part of the island; he could have gone ahead without consulting them, but it would have been a bad beginning. The boys would be fishing and working among the island men, living in the dormitory Cyrus had built near his own home. It was important that they not be made to feel as if they were resented.

The campers started with a clean slate on Coranoke. At the end of their stay, most of them had made friends among the villagers, and even earned their respect, which, in turn, gave the boys a measure of self-respect.

It was four days since Delle had left. Cyrus had caught up on more chores in those four days than he'd managed to accomplish in the past month. It hadn't helped. She was still as vivid in his mind as ever.

How long before the image began to fade?

He'd called Cromer and talked him into ferrying her across the inlet, and then he'd picked her up and driven her to the dock, intending to leave her there. Neither of them had found much to say.

What else could he have said? He'd told her that he needed her. More than once he'd asked her to stay, and it hadn't made any difference. She'd shut him out as effectively as if she'd slammed a door in his face when she'd offered to pay him for his services. He could have strangled her for that, but after he'd had time to cool off, he'd understood. Sort of.

Even if she cared—and he was almost certain she did—she was probably as scared as he was. Afraid to bring it out into the open because of the problems involved. Because it was too soon, too crazy. People didn't look at each other along the length of a twenty-foot ladder at six-fifteen in the morning and fall in love.

Did they?

They might as well have been strangers on the brief ride to the harbor. He'd considered running her across the inlet himself, but he hadn't trusted himself. She probably wouldn't have gone with him, anyway.

"Cromer's pumping out now. He'll be ready in a few minutes. Last chance for a free vacation on the sunny sands of Coranoke."

She'd passed up the opportunity for a crack at the weather. "No thanks. I have a long drive tonight and an early flight tomorrow."

Determined not to let it end on an inconclusive note, he'd tried again. "Honey, I don't know how to break it to you, but there aren't any drum in the Hudson River, and the beachcombing is lousy."

"Too bad. Next time I'll try Bimini—meanwhile, I'm meeting with representatives from four different banks in the next two days, and if I still have any energy left, I'll fly on down to Atlanta for a few more interviews after that."

"Hedging your bets, huh?" he suggested bitterly. Pulling up at the ramshackle fish house, he cut the engine.

"Look, you don't have to wait," Delle said hurriedly.

Cyrus tried to engage her eyes, but she turned away from him, fumbling with the door latch. Dammit, he'd known it wasn't going to be easy, but she wasn't even going to give them a chance!

Like an ever-present heartbeat, the muffled roar of the surf struck her as soon as she opened the door of the truck.

"Delle, wait."

Unable to help herself, she glanced over her shoulder, hoping the light was too dim for him to see her watering eyes. "Don't bother to get out, Cyrus, I can get my bag out of the back. Thanks for all—"

"Christ!" He jerked open his door and came around to where she stood, planting himself between her and the shadowy white boats lined up along the three plank dock. "Delle, wait a minute. There's something I have to say before you go."

Frantically, he composed and discarded a dozen statements, beginning with his net assets and his rather complex situation, and ending with a simple declaration of love. He decided against the first. If she wanted him, she'd have to take him as he was now, not as he'd been before.

"Delle, my mother was a summer woman. It's a term they use these days for the sort of woman who comes down here looking for a good time. She found her good time and she married him. My father. I reckon she thought it was romantic. She was bored with her own social set and not qualified for much else, and I guess my father was something new in her life. He owned the largest fishing boat around, and four houses. He liked to build houses, and he had plenty of land from both sides of his family."

Delle felt the cracks in her fragile armor begin to widen. She couldn't stay—she just couldn't! No matter how right it felt now, it could never work. She'd known Peter all her life. They'd come from the same background, and that hadn't worked. No matter how wonderful he was, Cyrus and she were an incredibly bad risk. All the odds were against it. No matter what he thought of her now, he'd soon be disappointed if she stayed. She wasn't one of those strong, stoic women he'd told her about, she was a city person. She couldn't even cook, much less mend nets.

Cyrus watched the expressions move across her face like fast moving cloud shadows. He knew what she was thinking—hell, he'd had doubts, too. The odds had been against them from the first, but what could he do? He was hooked. With a grim oath, he caught her to him and pressed his mouth against hers, releasing her before he could change his mind about letting her go. "Delle, I can't keep you here, but—"

"Cyrus, we've been over all that. I'm—I..." Placing a hand over her forehead, Delle shook her head. She was acting rationally for the first time since she got here. Maybe she'd better leave it at that.

The buzz of an electric pump that had gone unnoticed suddenly ceased. A moment later came the bubbling throb of a marine exhaust. Turning away, Cyrus lifted her suitcase from the bed of his truck and led the way to a boat that looked very much like his own. "Cromer, your passenger, Delle Richardson. Delle, Cromer Williams." He hopped aboard with the luggage, stowed it securely and then helped Delle down into the cockpit.

"You're not—"

"Going with you?" he finished for her. Cyrus shook his head. "No, I'm not. But Delle..." He took her hand so that she couldn't turn away. "Don't make me wait too long, will you? I'm not a patient man."

That night he'd come closer to drinking himself into oblivion than he had since the night when vandals had destroyed two-thirds of his art collection. Sprawled on the leather-covered couch in his den, he'd stared at a small bronze and thought about another one—the Giacometti that reminded him of Delle. It had been repairable, but he'd long since given it away. It had been too painful a reminder of something he'd done his best to put out of his mind. His collection.

With a growing and well-balanced portfolio, Cyrus had gone into collecting art purely as an investment. Like all brokers, whether or not they cared to admit it, he knew that art was one of the best investments available. What he *hadn't* known about was the inherent trap.

The trouble with good art was that it touched you where you lived. It spoke a subliminal language that needed no interpreters, and he'd grown far too attached to his paintings and sculptures, ever to consider selling.

Three boys with spray paint and knives had brought him to his knees. He'd left his apartment unlocked one evening to step down the hall and look at a watercolor a neighbor had just purchased. It had been a lousy painting, and Cyrus had accepted a drink while he tried to frame a tactful comment. Ten minutes, fifteen at most. He'd managed to come up with a suitably ambiguous critique, and then he'd gone back home and walked in on a nightmare in progress.

The hurt had gone too deep for revenge. It was the sheer senselessness of it that had all but crippled him. Professionals, heisting the stuff for a profit—that wouldn't have cut so deeply. He'd have been outraged, sure, but at least he'd have known that his collection had found another home with someone who respected it, if not for the right reasons.

It was shortly after that that the seeds of Camp Reliance had been sown. Before they'd been taken in custody, Cyrus had confronted the three vandals, the youngest about nine, the oldest no more than fourteen.

"Why?" he'd asked.

The oldest one had shrugged. The other two had stared at their paint-stained sneakers. Not one of them had come up with an answer, even when they'd been taken away by a uniformed policeman and someone from juvenile.

Cyrus's carefully constructed security, the comfortable world he'd built for himself, had begun to collapse at that moment, triggered by what he'd seen in their eyes. Not shame, certainly not remorse. Fear, resentment, hostility and something else—something that had touched him in a way that nothing else ever had.

Hell, they were just babies! At their age he'd been canoeing and backpacking at some fancy place his mother had picked out, or here on Coranoke with his father, fishing, hunting, eating raw oysters and briny corned mullet and drinking boiled coffee diluted with canned milk.

It had taken a while, but in the end, Cyrus had known what he had to do. No way could he have crawled back into his comfortable cocoon and gone on collecting art, clipping coupons, playing mixed doubles at the club and writing tidy little checks to various charities now and then to salve his conscience.

Even after settling his business affairs, he'd put in more than a year just getting ready, taking courses in subjects he'd never even heard of before, reading stacks of books, conferring with social services from county up to state level. There had been an unbelievable amount of red tape involved, but it had been worth every hour of frustration he'd put in.

Cyrus could truthfully say that not once since he'd moved back to Coranoke to take over the property he'd inherited had he regretted the move. He'd visited the island at least once a year for as long as his father had lived. He knew everyone on Coranoke and most of the people on the other two islands, as well. He was probably kin to about half of them on his father's side.

His mother, remarried and still living in Charlotte, had encouraged him to return to Coranoke. The daughter of a physician, she hadn't been able to take the isolation on the island, but she'd never resented his love for his father's home. Now that there were state-operated ferries, the place wasn't even all that isolated anymore.

Still, for someone like Delle... Cordell Richardson's daughter would have led an even more sheltered life than his mother had before she'd struck out on her own. Unfortunately, Delle had struck out in the wrong direction.

Cyrus groaned. As if he weren't suffering enough, he had to drink himself into a king-size hangover. Real smart.

But it had hurt unbearably to see her standing there in the stern of Cromer's boat as it pulled away from the dock. He hadn't planned to linger, but he'd been helpless...watching that slight, proud figure grow smaller and smaller, with no guarantee that he'd ever see her again.

Delle paid the toll to get her car out of hock as another incoming jet screamed over the airport's long-term parking lot. Her head was splitting, and she felt travel stained. Too miserable even to go through the hassle of changing her reservations, she'd stayed on the extra day, even though she'd canceled her other two appointments.

Then, in a fit of restlessness, she'd gone on a shopping spree. Stretching her credit to the limit, she'd bought things she didn't need and couldn't afford, and now she was furious with herself.

Why on earth had she done it? In spite of her father's indulgence—or perhaps because of it—shopping had never been an addiction of hers. Her wardrobe was as precisely planned as every other facet of her life. Each season, she updated it with a few accessories and one major purchase.

So why had she gone wild on Fifth Avenue? She didn't even like most of what she'd bought, she'd simply gone on a binge. Now not only was her budget shot, her conscience was giving her the devil. She hadn't behaved so irresponsibly since the time her father put her on a plane to New York just before he and the boys took off on another flight for a hunting lodge in Colorado. His trip had been by way of a last fling, just three weeks before he'd married Jeanette.

"What I need is sleep," she told herself. Two aspirin, two antacids, a long, hot bath and twenty-four hours of sleep. After that, she'd decide where she was going from there.

* * *

"Daniel, it wasn't my *fault*! Henderson's the type who'd stick pins in little dolls and leave them hidden in people's desks, and—"

She held the phone away from her ear and waited impatiently. "All right, so I'm exaggerating. We just didn't like each other. He completely ignored the fact that they were the ones who approached me in the first place."

"What about Federal Mercantile? You didn't care for the decor?" Daniel's sarcasm came through the line quite clearly, and Delle hung on to her patience by a thread. She knew he'd counted on making the move to New York with her. Daniel had been personnel's idea of a joke—the firm's first male secretary for the first female executive—but they'd hit it off from the beginning.

"The decor was early Rothschild," she said with a heavy sigh. "And Mrs. Kolodny was lovely. Unfortunately, someone upstairs screwed up, and the position I was supposed to be interviewed for had already been filled." Wrapped in a towel, her hair dripping down her back, she patted her bare foot on the white carpet. "I'm still on my vacation, in case you've forgotten," she said pointedly.

"How's your stomach been behaving?"

"Fine!" she screeched. "Just fine, now would you please let me get some clothes on? I have a plane to catch in exactly two and a half hours, and I haven't even unpacked from New York."

Atlanta was no better. Delle hadn't expected it to be, but she went through the motions, giving the most lackluster interviews of her career. The weather couldn't have been lovelier, the sky that deep shade of sapphire that epitomizes autumn. The leaves had hung on longer than usual, and amid Atlanta's eclectic business architecture, incandescent touches of scarlet, orange and gold fluttered like lacy banners.

All around her were signs of a growing economy, a city on the move, and Delle didn't care. She simply didn't care any longer, and it was all *his* fault.

Back in Norfolk, she threw herself into her work, taking on more than her share, tackling the toughest prospects with grim determination. Along with everyone else, she courted insanity as file after file was lost in the voracious maw of the wonderful new computer system.

She ate erratically and yelled at Daniel when he fussed over her. "I don't *need* to be fed! If I'm hungry, I'll eat. Now take that mess away and see if you can get that one-eyed monster to spit out the Tolliver-Tidewater file. And call the comptroller's office at MidTown Developers and set up an appointment. The sooner the better, because First Federal's snapping at my heels on this one."

She cried a lot. Her nerves were ragged and her temper was beginning to interfere with her work, and she knew she couldn't go on this way. She called her father one Friday, and when he invited her to come for the weekend, Delle surprised herself by accepting.

Cordell was in his seventies now. He looked ten years younger. The ivy that covered the gray stone Georgian house was as lush and green as ever, the grounds as beautifully maintained. Jeanette had let her hair go natural, and the gray was becoming. Delle told her so.

"You're looking good, too, Delle," her stepmother said.

"I've had a vacation." A vacation that had haunted her every hour since she'd been back. Delle tried to picture Cyrus against the background of her father's home. Surprisingly, he fit in quite well. "As a matter of fact," she went on, "I saw Oren and Peter while I was there. They were on a fishing trip with one of Oren's prospects."

Cordell Richardson brought drinks, his own well watered on the advice of his physician, and settled into the

chair Delle used to think of as his throne. Either the chair
had grown larger or the king had grown smaller...or her
perspective had changed.

"You know, it could be that I was wrong about you and
Peter, Cordelia. He's a sound enough man, a good, church-
going Republican." Delle nearly strangled on her drink at
that point. "All the same," her father went on, "I'm not
sure you didn't need a stronger hand on the reins than he'd
have provided."

"Now, Cordell," Jeanette murmured. Keeping an un-
easy eye on Delle, she reached out to pat her husband pla-
catingly on the arm. "I'm sure we're all just as proud of
Delle as we can be, aren't we? Is that your second drink or
your third, dear? I lost count."

All in all, Delle decided on the way home, it had been a
good visit. Somewhere along the way, she seemed to have
lost the old defensiveness that had once pitted her against
every member of her family.

Delle felt a sense of achievement in having come to terms
with the past, but there was one effect she hadn't counted
on. With nothing to prove and no one to prove it to, her
priorities were beginning to resettle into a disturbing new
pattern.

On Monday night she went out to dinner and a show with
a man she'd dated occasionally. She turned down his invitation for the following night. On Wednesday night she took
in an art opening with another male friend. Warmed by too
many champagne cocktails, she made the mistake of invit-
ing him in for coffee after he brought her home, and ended
up having to throw him out when he mistook the invitation
for something more.

On Thursday, she had a note from June with an apology
for the latest attempt at matchmaking and a promise never,
ever to meddle again. Delle laughed in spite of the familiar
prickling at the back of her eyes, and then she went on to

read the rest of the note. There was a recipe for the world's best coconut cake and a snapshot of June's six-year-old in her Brownie uniform.

"A recipe? Oh, June, you conniving witch, you never give up, do you?" June had majored in Home Ec. She'd known from the ninth grade on, exactly what she wanted out of life.

On Friday, Delle got back the pictures she'd taken at Coranoke. Without access to a darkroom, she'd had to rely on a commercial developer, and she'd harbored an abiding fear that he'd lose them, leaving her nothing to show for her time at Coranoke.

Nothing except a heart that wouldn't stop aching and a head that wouldn't stop dreaming.

It was all there—the pelicans with their comical solemnity, the neat clutter of boats and nets that surrounded the houses. She'd never even seen where Cyrus lived.

"Oh, my palm tree," she crooned, peering at the unsightly swollen trunk with its three yellowed fronds. Her eyes blurred. Dear Lord, when was it going to stop hurting?

Ten

The first week of the new year had almost ended before Delle was able to get away. It had taken her that long, even with the addition of vacation time, to work out her notice. Daniel had been stunned, hurt, and angry, in that order, but Delle had gone to bat for him in the inevitable shuffle that would result from her leaving. His anger had quickly dissipated when he learned that he was to be secretary to the senior vice president. He had already bought a five foot tall schefflera for his new office.

On the eighth day of January she locked her door, hurried out to her car and prayed that the threatening snow would hold off until she was far enough south and east to escape it.

And prayed that she wasn't making the landmark mistake of her life. The cold feet she was experiencing weren't entirely due to the twenty-six-degree temperature.

Delle had planned to spend the night at a motel in Hatteras and cross to Coranoke on the first ferry, leaving herself plenty of time to get back if things felt strange. She'd made her plans carefully, and it had all sounded reasonable enough at first—a post-holiday vacation, an impromptu drive down to the Outer Banks. Nothing extraordinary about that.

Just thought I'd revisit the scene of the crime, she'd say airily. No—scratch that. Maybe something about fishing, about the big one that got away. She groaned and braked for a stoplight. It wasn't too late to back out, she reminded herself, knowing that nothing short of a blizzard could hold her back now.

Once before she'd found herself in an impossible situation, one that could lead only to disaster. From a source beyond her understanding, she'd found the courage to do what had to be done, and she'd never once regretted it.

This time, she might not be so lucky. What if she'd misread Cyrus's meaning? What if he wasn't there? He'd warned her that he wasn't a patient man. Worse still, what if he looked at her as if he couldn't quite place her and said, "Don't tell me—Deb, isn't it? No, Dottie. You were here last summer, right?"

Delle's stomach gave an unpleasant lurch. She'd have to stop somewhere and get something for it. She never made New Year's resolutions, but this time, in an impulsive gesture, she'd sworn off antacids and flushed away her entire supply. Meanwhile, positive thinking would have to suffice.

"It'll be all right," she reassured herself. "It has to be."

Slate-gray clouds sagged low as she neared the village of Hatteras. From atop a cupola near the sound side, a red pennant whipped in the wind. Small craft warnings. Was a ferry considered a small craft? What if it wasn't running?

Acting on impulse, Delle passed the motel where she'd intended to spend the night and headed for the ferry landing. It was nowhere near five-thirty, but she dared not take a chance. The thought of being stuck here on Hatteras, with Coranoke so near, yet utterly inaccessible, brought dampness to the palms of her hands. Why didn't they bridge the damned inlet? Then she wouldn't have to go through this agony!

The ferry was at the slip, ramp down and barrier arm raised. She pulled up to scan the information sign and discovered that the winter schedule was now in effect. Two runs a day, leaving this side at nine-thirty a.m. and three-thirty p.m.

Two things happened at once. A man clad in yellow oilskins waved her aboard, and a red pickup pulled up behind her and began to honk impatiently. Without time to think, Delle found herself creeping up the ramp and taking her place between a rusty station wagon and a fish truck.

So much for all her careful planning. She peered through a windshield already beginning to haze over at the wild gray seascape. It was exhilarating. Whitecaps raced furiously past, crashing against every obstacle. Overhead, sea gulls banked and hovered on the fierce wind, sharp white accents against a forbidding sky.

Delle rolled down her window a scant three inches as her view was obscured by salt spray. "Wind 'bout blowed all the water across to Englehard," the cheerful attendant yelled to her as he chocked her wheels. "Reckon we'll kiss the bottom more 'n' once 'tween here 'n' Corn'oke. Tide falls any lower, might not even run tomorrow."

Talk about blind instinct, Delle marveled, what else would have made her hand in her resignation a week after she'd got back from Atlanta? What else would have brought her to the Outer Banks just in time to make what might be the last ferry for days? What had led her directly to the ferry instead of allowing her to stop at the motel, as she'd planned?

All right, so it had been a ferry attendant and an impatient driver behind her who were directly responsible for her being on board at this moment; she preferred to think of it as fate.

The ride seemed interminable. The small, sturdy vessel pitched and groaned its way across the inlet, and Delle soon discovered what the man had meant by "kissing the bottom." At dead low tide, with a following wind rolling the heavy seas beneath the steel hull, they snagged sandbar after sandbar, and she had visions of spending the night in the middle of Hatteras Inlet, within sight of both islands, out of reach of either.

The landing was even rougher than the short voyage had been, with the wind catching them broadside and swinging them against the pilings time after time. By the time she was free to disembark, she was almost seasick. As for her lovely new car, it had been thoroughly splashed with saltwater and was probably already beginning to rust.

"So be it," she muttered, gunning the engine and creeping up the narrow plank ramp.

Barely four o'clock, and already it was nearly dark. Despite the efficiency of her heater, Delle's feet were frozen. Now that she was actually here, what next? Where did she go?

On Coranoke, where *was* there to go?

This had been a mistake, a bad mistake. She should have stuck to her original plans, checking into a motel and calling Cyrus from there. She could have mentioned casually that she was vacationing at Hatteras and left the next move up to him. Now, thanks to an eager-beaver ferry attendant and a driver who couldn't wait for her to pull out of line, she'd landed herself on his doorstep uninvited, and there

was no going back. Worse, she had no assurance, other than
this erratic instinct of hers, that he really wanted her.

"I'll be waiting," he'd said, but talk was cheap. He'd
probably felt pretty safe at the time. After all, what idiot
would throw away a career like hers on the basis of a brief
romance?

"This idiot," Delle muttered, pulling into the driveway
beside the battered palm tree. But it was the time they'd had
together, plus weeks of soul-searching that had led her to the
realization that without Cyrus, nothing in her life would
have meaning.

The cottage was dark, the storm shutters closed, and she
didn't know why she'd gone there in the first place. Possibly because it was the only place she knew on the island, and
before she set out to find Cyrus, she needed to get her bearings.

Did it really belong to Cyrus, or had he been trying to
impress her? He didn't strike her as the type of man who'd
go out of his way to make an impression on anyone. Why
should he? In ragged sneakers and torn-off jeans, the
impression he'd made on her was more profound than anything she'd ever experienced in her life. Whatever the roof
he slept under, at least it wouldn't leak. Cyrus knew how to
do things.

But then, so did she. She'd proved that much over the
past six years. Surely she could learn to catch fish and crabs
and oysters and clams. If she set her mind to it, she could
even learn to cook the blasted things.

Time enough later to dig out her cookbook, Delle told
herself as she tucked her icy fingers under her arms for
warmth. If she sat here much longer, the whole matter of her
abilities—or lack of them—would be academic. She
couldn't cower here in the darkness much longer without
getting frostbite. Cyrus had told her once that his was the

only house on the sound side. She couldn't remember if that was Out or Over, but she was fairly certain that if she took a left at the crossroad, she'd eventually find it.

As it turned out, the house proved easy enough to find, though larger than she'd expected. For a moment Delle thought she might have made a mistake, but there was the Blazer. And a boat. And a mountain of silvery nets, and a stack of crab pots. But no lights anywhere.

Seriously alarmed by now, Delle got out of her car and hurried to the shelter of the porch. Something cold and wet was falling, either sleet or snow, but she ignored it.

God, had everyone deserted this place? Did the whole island, like so many of the businesses she'd passed on her way down the banks, close down between Thanksgiving and Easter? What had happened to the people who'd crossed over on the ferry with her? Swallowed up by quicksand?

Cupping her hands around her eyes, Delle tried to peer inside, but it was no use. The windows were filthy, as if no one had washed them in years.

"Hang on and I'll turn on a light so you can see better."

The deep, raspy drawl came from behind her, and Delle's heart flung itself against her ribs like a wild bird newly caged. "Cyrus, where did you—I thought everyone—"

"Come on inside and warm up," he invited.

Wishing with all her heart she'd never embarked on this reckless, ill-advised odyssey, she followed him inside to where it was warm and dry, and then stood rooted just inside the door, unable to lift her face for fear he'd be able to read every thought in her head. Miserably ill at ease, she said the first thing that came into her head. "Your windows are a mess."

"Salt film. Can't fight it. When did you get in?"

"Just now. I—uh, was at Hatteras and I thought I'd run over here to see how you were getting along." It was literally true, she told herself.

"I guess you know you've missed the last ferry back."

Delle found the courage to raise her eyes and then wished she'd kept them on the floor. Even loving him until she ached with it, she'd forgotten just how magnificent he was. Hip boots furled above his knees, straps dangling, lent him a piratical look, and winter had whipped a rosy hue into his lean, tanned features, making his eyes startlingly green by contrast. He was hatless, but he wore an oilskin slicker, open now to reveal a navy flannel shirt with a wedge of thermal underwear showing at the throat.

She began to smile, and then to laugh.

"Delle?"

Neither of them had moved. They were standing just inside the door in a small foyer. The paneled walls sported a coatrack filled with an assortment of garments, including a pair of waders. Over the door, a rack of antlers held two hats, neither of which she could imagine Cyrus wearing. The floor was covered in nondescript vinyl, and that was dotted with several well-worn rag rugs.

"Have you eaten?"

She shook her head. "Not since breakfast," she admitted breathlessly.

"At least you're eating breakfast these days."

Tension sharpened his features, fractured the light in his eyes. Delle found that she was holding her breath. *He's afraid of me! He thinks I'm expecting something from him...a commitment?*

Deserted by her courage now that it was much too late, she shut her eyes. She'd done it again—misread every signal, barged in at the wrong place, the wrong time, and now she had to get out of here before she fell apart completely.

"Delle." His voice was low, but quite audible. "If you don't get out of my house and off this island in thirty seconds flat—"

I *knew* it, she wailed inwardly.

"—you can kiss your precious career goodbye, because you won't be leaving here. If I have to burn every damned boat in the harbor, yank out the phones and blow up the ferries, I'll keep you here."

Much later, Delle lay beside him in the iron bed in which his father had been born and toyed with the flattened curls that patterned his chest. "I've never been so scared in all my life," she confessed.

"Not even when you told a church full of people that they were welcome to go to the reception, and while they were there they could collect their wedding gifts, because there wouldn't be a wedding after all?"

"Not even then." She kissed one dusky flat disk for the sheer thrill of watching it tighten into a tiny stud before her eyes. Since the time he'd caught her to him, fish scales, icy oilskins and all, and kissed her to within an inch of unconsciousness, she'd come a long way.

She'd learned, for instance, that no matter how strong a man appears to be, he's as subject to doubts and uncertainties as any woman. She'd learned that the strength and stability she'd sensed in Cyrus had not been an illusion. It was those very qualities that had enabled him to rise above a senseless act of violence, to reexamine his values and redirect his whole life.

Surely she could rise above her family's misdirected efforts to see her safely married, and her own efforts at earning her independence. Hadn't they been equally misdirected? She'd been hurt and frightened at the time, but even so, she'd quickly regained her balance and gone on from there. She'd proved something to herself, and to her family, as well.

"Couldn't you have given me a hint?" she asked now.

"That I loved you, or the other?"

"About anything! At first I couldn't imagine why a man of your obvious intelligence was hiding himself away down here doing odd jobs and fishing. You must have laughed over that."

"Love, I'll admit to laughing at you once or twice, but not over that. Never over the important things. How could I have told you? And what? That I owned enough in the way of securities and real estate to keep the wolf from the door? How would that have sounded?"

"Well, about your camp, at least."

"You wouldn't have questioned it? You wouldn't have wondered how and why I'd gotten involved in such a project? Come on, sweetheart, you'd have started asking questions, and first thing you know, the whole thing would have come tumbling out. I wouldn't have had any secrets, including the way I felt about you."

"Would that have been so awful?" Delle whispered.

A wave of something that looked almost like pain washed across Cyrus's face and was gone. "Love makes demands," he said, his voice a shade deeper, rougher. "No man has the right to make such a demand of any woman. You've invested six years of your life in something, Delle. The fact that I think it was a bad investment doesn't give me the right to ask you to throw it away. I told you once that life here can be hard on a woman. It forces you to face some basic truths about who you are, and some people aren't ready for that."

"I've already faced the most important truth, Cyrus, by coming back."

"It takes a strong woman to make it here. There aren't any shops, no theaters, no bridge parties or night clubs."

"Instead, there are sunsets over the Pamlico Sound, moonrises over the Atlantic Ocean, blue herons and pelicans, acres of brown rushes that turn silvery when the wind sweeps over them, and miles of untouched beaches to be explored."

"Some of the finest people you'll meet anywhere in the world," he put in. "And the mainland isn't all that far away. We'll check in now and then just to be sure it's still there. Summers there's swimming, surfing, sailing—that is, if you don't mind sharing our time with a flock of boys."

"Not all of it, I hope," Delle said pointedly. They were lying under a down-filled comforter in the paneled bedroom. Over the iron bed was a magnificent oil of the marshes at dawn.

"Greedy little beggar, aren't you? If you'll set up photography classes for the boys in the summertime, I'll teach you to be a fisherman's wife when summer's over. You still haven't caught that trophy drum, remember?"

"I don't need any trophies, not any more. But I never back down from a challenge. If I can learn business math, I can certainly manage to teach photography. We have a long, hard winter to get through first, though," she said softly, her fingers beginning to stray in teasing circles on his naked skin. "I could use a few more lessons in my wifely duties."

With a groan, Cyrus caught her and pulled her on top of him. "More lessons? After all I've taught you already?"

"The bathtub lessons didn't count," Delle said primly. "I wasn't ready."

He laughed aloud. "Honey, if you'd been any more ready, we'd both have gone down the drain."

"Oh, Cyrus, what if I hadn't found you?" Delle whispered suddenly. "Do you realize the mathematical odds against our ever meeting?'' Wrapping both arms tightly about him, she buried her face in his throat, savoring the warmth, the clean, musky scent of his body.

"With friends like yours?'' he scoffed. ''Honey, I don' think you give them the credit they deserve. Are we going to invite them to the wedding?''

"Invite them? I hadn't even made up my mind to *tell* them about it. Do you know what they did to us?''

"Yeah, and their efforts on your behalf finally paid off didn't they? What do you think, shall we name our first born after them?''

"Cyrus J. H. P. Burrus. I don't know, darling—it's a lot to saddle a boy with. How about a free week's vacation at one of your cottages every summer?''

"I think we can handle that.'' His hands slipped down over her back to press her against him, and Delle's breath caught in her throat. ''Meanwhile, you mentioned this insatiable thirst for knowledge you've acquired.''

"Another lesson? Really?''

"It's been a long time, darling,'' he whispered, passion and laughter bringing a familiar gleam to his narrowed eyes. "Like everything else around here, I'm a bit rusty, but I'l do my level best.''

"It's been half an hour, and there's not a speck of rust on you anywhere,'' Delle declared. ''Believe me, if there were I'd have discovered it by now.''

Cyrus laughed wholeheartedly. ''I'm beginning to see how you managed to get so far in a field you were wildly un suited for. When you set out to do something, you don't foo around, do you?''

"Seriously, Cyrus, I'm not going to be much help to you at first. I can't cook, I can't do things with nets, I don' know the first thing about little boys—'' Her legs were en twined with his and she was trapped.

Cyrus held her upper body just far enough away so that he could watch the play of emotions on her face. "I can cook," he said gruffly. "I'll teach you to line net if you really want to learn, and little boys aren't all that different from big ones. We have counselors to oversee everything. The boys'll fish and crab-pot with me, and you can knock off a few of the rough edges with your photography classes, and of course, they'll all fall in love with you, but that'll be good for them, too. Give 'em something to live up to. Any more questions?"

"Do I get my own darkroom?"

"This one's not dark enough for you?"

"Depends on what you had in mind." She knew precisely what he had in mind. Lying on her side, Delle slipped her leg between his thighs and snuggled closer. "We could turn off the lights and see what develops."

"Delle—" Cyrus, his voice oddly thickened, sought her eyes. "I'd have come after you if you hadn't come back when you did."

"Would you have?" She felt her heart expand wildly inside her.

"They say you can't fall in love at first sight, and maybe they're right, but if that's the case, I've loved you in another lifetime and been searching for you all this time." His words, spoken in that husky whisper, touched off a response deep inside her, and Delle could only cling to him. "I recognized you, you know. Something happened to me when I looked down from that ladder and saw you standing there—it just took me a while to catch on to what it was."

"Cyrus—oh, Cyrus. I never dreamed it was possible to love someone this much. Why did I waste so much of our precious time?"

His lips brushed her eyelids shut, while his hands began to feather their magic over her body, tantalizing each secret cache of pleasure with a hint of delights to come. "Nothing's wasted, love," he murmured. "We've all the time in the world."

As the ageless ritual began once more, Delle sighed, a soft shuddering sound that was lost in the creaking of old timbers. The house braced itself against the fury of another winter.

 Silhouette Desire

COMING NEXT MONTH

RAGE OF PASSION—Diana Palmer
When Maggie fled from her ex-husband to Texas, she never expected to find an ally in Gabriel, her childhood enemy. Could their feelings flare into love?

MADAM'S ROOM—Jennifer Greene
The joint inheritance of a mansion with an illicit history brought Margaret and Mike together. The house inspired her secret fantasies, but Mike convinced her that his love was sweeter than dreams.

THE MAN AT IVY BRIDGE—Suzanne Forster
Years ago Chloe had seen a mysterious man near her estate, the same week that her step sister disappeared. Could Nathanial be the phantom who'd left his mark on her heart?

PERFECT TIMING—Anna Cavaliere
Olivia had only requested Jonas for an evening, and he played the role of her husband perfectly. But Jonas had other ideas and was determined to make their "marriage" real.

YESTERDAY'S LOVE—Sherryl Woods
The IRS had sent Tate to audit the books of Victoria's antique shop and her complete lack of organization drove him wild. But it soon became clear that opposites do attract!

NEVADA SILVER—Joan Hohl
The third book in Joan Hohl's trilogy for Desire: Kit Aimsley, the half sister of the hero of *California Copper* (Desire #312), and Logan McKittrick— a man she's known all her life—discover the love they share.

AVAILABLE NOW:

TOO HOT TO HANDLE
Elizabeth Lowell

LADY LIBERTY
Naomi Horton

A FAIR BREEZE
Ann Hurley

TO MEET AGAIN
Lass Small

BROOKE'S CHANCE
Robin Elliott

A WINTER WOMAN
Dixie Browning

Coming February
from Special Editions—
The final book in Nora Roberts's sensational
MacGregor Series

For Now, Forever

The MacGregor Series, published in 1985, followed the
lives and loves of the MacGregor children. We were
inundated with fan mail—and one request stood out:
Tell us about Daniel and Anna's romance!

For Now, Forever is that Story...

Anna is a proud, independent woman determined
against all odds to be a surgeon. Daniel is ambitious
and arrogant, a self-made tycoon who wants a woman
to share his home and raise his children. Together they
battle each other and their feelings as they try to make
their own dreams come true.

Look for *Playing the Odds*, *Tempting Fate*, *All the
Possibilities* and *One Man's Art*, all to be reissued in
February in a special Collectors Edition.

Don't miss them wherever paperbacks are sold.